I0547791

X and Complicated Rhythms

Eugene Rookwood

Dexcel Publishing * Indianapolis, Indiana

X *and* Complicated Rhythms

ISBN 978-0-9704015-0-2

Printed in the United States of America

The brutal truth can be devastating...
yet very liberating...

Eugene Rookwood

Chapter one

Kenneth *Weber squirmed* and pretended to be asleep. His wife, Marsha was awake and aroused. She was making sexual advances but Kenneth wasn't really interested and Marsha knew it. She settled down and stared at the ceiling wondering what had gone wrong sexually. They were into their fifth year of a childless marriage and their sex life, which had never been great, has all but disappeared. During the first few weeks of their marriage they could hardly keep their bodies apart, but that broiling heat quickly cooled to slow cook, then to simmer, to barely warm, to occasional drunken horny lust relief sessions, to now. And practically nothing happens now.

In fact, Marsha thought, the only occasional bright spot in their sex lives seems to follow Kenneth's fishing trips with his old college roommate David. Kenneth comes home horny and their sex life is great for a short while then rapidly declines. "This makes no sense!" Marsha spoke aloud, "Our marriage is nearly perfect in every other way so there has to be a reason for our nonexistent sex life. And...if there is a reason, then there must also be a solution." She looked at Kenneth who was now really asleep. "The reason or problem that is screwing up our sex lives is not in my head so it must be in yours sweetheart and I am going to get to the bottom of this. I promise you that…" she whispered then lightly kissed Kenneth before turning over and going to sleep.

The next morning Marsha confronted him. "What's happening to us Ken? Why is nothing going on?" she demanded. "Why are you no longer interested in me sexually? You're not…it's obvious so you are not going to hurt my feelings by saying it."

"Marsha…look if we try and get into this now I am going to be late for work and so are you. Can we shelve this until after dinner?" Kenneth pleaded.

"Why not! Our sex life has been on the shelf for years!" Marsha countered.

"We'll talk, I promise," Kenneth offered as he hurried from the house.

Feeling agitated Marsha watched him go, but even while at work she spent most of the day thinking about her marriage and sex life. She was in a determined mood and well prepared that same evening after dinner when she poured two glasses of straight scotch and again confronted Kenneth. "So are you now ready to talk about what's happening…or really what's not happening with our sex lives?" she asked.

"Whadda you mean…what's happening with our sex lives?" Kenneth responded. "We have sex…same as everybody else!"

"Oh come on Kenneth!" Marsha shot back. "That's a crock and you know it! Once every two weeks maybe…and sometimes it's a month or more! Don't tell me we have sex just like everybody else or even like we use to. The only time we have good sex is after one of your dumb fishing trips with David."

"That's not true!" Kenneth snapped.

"Yes it is!" Marsha insisted. "You always come back from those trips horny. I think being with no one but your old college roommate makes you miss me and I wish you would go fishing more often."

"I'd love too but David's wife seldom lets him go," Kenneth sighed.

"I didn't know David was such a wimp," Marsha pouted.

"Well...hey they got two kids you know and he is trying to make his marriage work!" Kenneth responded defensively then added, "Cyndi is a difficult woman...you've never met her have you?"

"Of course I met her! I met her at our wedding and again when we visited them two years ago," Marsha reminded him.

"Then you know how difficult she is. Damn shame too!" Kenneth grumbled. "I'd love to be at the lake fishing."

"Can't go by yourself huh?" Marsha questioned.

"That would be about as much fun as bowling a perfect game by yourself!" Kenneth groused.

"What do you guys do up in the woods...all by yourselves? Huh? Just exactly what do you do?" Marsha demanded.

"Whadda you mean...what do we do? We fish...then clean em...cook 'em and eat 'em. Then maybe fish some more or hunt some or relax, drink beer, talk a little...you know guy stuff," Kenneth explained.

"No Kenneth, I don't know!" Marsha snapped. "Tell me just what guy stuff is? What's happening in those woods that makes you horny for me?"

"Oh come on Marsha, I don't even know what you are talking about," Kenneth insisted. "I don't remember being especially horny after a fishing trip."

"Kenneth!" Marsha shrieked. "How can you not remember? It's the only time our sex life is worth remembering."

"Okay! Okay...enough already," Kenneth pleaded. "I don't know the answer. Maybe being away from it all, deep in the woods...at the lake...you know...maybe that just invigorates me."

Anxiety hung in the air as Marsha refilled their glasses with scotch. Both of them knew the conversation would now get deeper. And both of them also knew Marsha would get the complete and total truth from her husband's mouth so both took long drinks from their glass.

The confession yet to come was long overdue. For months Marsha had avoided these very thoughts and refused to consider such possibilities. Now however, with her sex life seemingly dependent upon another man with whom her husband spent time alone, she could no longer stand not knowing and was determined to hear about everything they did.

"Kenneth!" Marsha began anew in a matter-of-fact tone. "I don't want to hear this clinical bullshit about the woods invigorating you. I've been to the woods with you and you didn't come back horny or invigorated. It's only when you go on those weekends with David that you come back horny and fun. I want to know exactly what you and David do that makes you that way. I want to know so you can do more of it. I like you that way."

"Do you really mean that?" Kenneth asked.

"Of course I mean that!" Marsha assured. "Honey...I'm your wife! I love you...and I absolutely love it when you are horny and want me. Whatever it takes to get you that way I'm all for it."

Kenneth was finding it hard to speak. His eyes filled with tears as he emptied his glass. "David and I go back a long way," he blurted out.

"I know sweetie," Marsha consoled.

"We were roomies in college...from the first day to the last David was my roomie," Kenneth continued.

"Uh-huh, I know," Marsha advised in a gentle voice.

Kenneth began to sniff as tears ran down his cheeks, he blew his nose then took another drink after Marsha refilled his glass. "Well...we fish and everything like I said... but...we wrestle some too," he confessed.

"You wrestle?" Marsha questioned.

"Yeah, pure wrestle."

"What is pure wrestle?"

"Look this is the only secret I've kept from you...I've never told anyone about this. David and I swore secrecy to each other and it's just not easy to talk about...okay?" Kenneth pleaded.

"I'm trying to understand honey, but why is wrestling such a big deal?" Marsha patiently inquired.

"We wrestle by the original rules of the ancient Greeks. True ancient Greco wrestling," Kenneth explained.

"And just exactly what are the rules of true ancient Greco wrestling?" Marsha questioned with great interest.

Kenneth again emptied his glass, he should have been drunk but wasn't. He wiped his eyes, sat upright and cleared his throat. "Ah...well..." he began, "ah two guys completely nude and heavily oiled wrestle, man against man, will against will until one is broken then conquered."

"And that's it?" Marsha asked.

"No not exactly...ah...ah the defeated man must honor his conqueror and submit," Kenneth explained.

"What do you mean submit?"

"Ah...ah the loser has to..." Kenneth flushed red as he revealed the truth. "Ah...ah the loser has to suck the winner."

"Suck the winner!" Marsha repeated in disbelief.

"Yeah...ah...you know."

"You mean suck his cock?" Marsha sharply questioned.

"Yes..." Kenneth admitted. "Those are the rules...that's what makes it such a powerful struggle. In ancient Greece the wrestling was done in public meets before huge crowds. Can you imagine the tremendous struggles that took place, the desperate determination, the adrenaline rush, the pride of winning or humiliation of losing...the pure excitement! I get a small piece of that when I wrestle with David," he concluded with obvious excitement.

"And you suck his cock when you lose?"

"Goddamnit! I told you this wasn't easy to talk about Marsha!" Kenneth snapped. "Those are the fucking rules...I didn't make them okay. If you are gonna wrestle by ancient Greco rules then you either win or suck cock."

"What happens after that?" Marsha inquired.

"Nothing, it's over."

"Just like that?"

"Yeah, just like that...soon as the victor gets off or pushes the loser away it's over!"

Marsha was disgusted yet intrigued. For a moment she felt numb. Had she been sober the marriage would now be in serious trouble. But, thanks to the liquor and a complete lack of sex, Marsha's body ruled this evening and it was demanding relief. She was wet, hot, very horny and had gotten swept up in the heat and intensity of this talk of naked oily men wrestling. She imagined their bodies sliding, grabbing, colliding and finally locked together in desperate confrontation with defeat and humiliation waiting for the loser. Suspecting there was more and determined to hear all of it, Marsha served snacks, refilled their glasses then snuggled onto the sofa. "Greco wrestling really sounds intense," she commented.

"It is!" Kenneth eagerly responded. "It's the ultimate test! Just you, totally naked, man against man...a battle for manhood. God it's so good."

"What if the loser refuses to suck?"

"Then by the rules the winner can take his life," Kenneth explained. "But in ancient Greece the crowd watching the match would probably attack a loser that refused and literally pull his limbs from his body. In college losers that refused got pissed on. But any guy really into ancient Greco knows the loser gains strength by sucking the essence from his conqueror.

"Ugh...that's yucky..." Marsha responded. "Tell me what it feels like to wrestle naked?"

"Jeez...I don't know...it feels great really," Kenneth replied.

"You guys get oiled up?"

"Of course you gotta...those are the rules...and we follow the rules to the letter," Kenneth answered.

"Tell me about your last match," Marsha responded.

"Whadda you mean? I mean whadda you want to know?"

"Everything!" Marsha insisted. "Come on Kenneth tell me all about it...you're getting a woody just thinking about it aren't cha?"

"Yeah."

"Well come on then tell me. Do you like the feel of your naked body rubbing against his?" Marsha teasingly questioned.

"Yeah..."

"Do you guys get hard-ons while you're wrestling?"

"Oh yeah...really powerful hard-ons!" Kenneth bragged. "It's really cool because you're not thinking about that...you're wrestling to win. But sometimes you make a move to get a hold and you feel your hard cock slide against his back or shoulder or down the crack of his ass. You feel it...or you feel his cock rubbing against you. Both guys get incredible hard-ons and that only makes the battle tougher...true man to man. You feel his chest heaving against yours...you feel him breathe...his muscles straining...but you can't get carried away with that because you will lose concentration and he'll throw you or worse."

"What's the worst?"

"Oh God, the head scissors!" Kenneth responded. "When you get a guys head between your thighs, your cock is right in his face. The thigh muscles are very powerful if you put enough pressure on his head and he can't break the hold, your opponent will lose his will to fight and surrender by opening his mouth and sucking your cock."

"Tell me about your last match."

"I lost!"

"I see...how long have you guys been wrestling like this?" Marsha asked.

"Since our second year of college?"

"Have you wrestled with any other guys?"

"A couple when I was in college," Kenneth responded.

"A couple?"

"Okay four, but I beat two of them."

"How often did you and David wrestle when you were in college?"

"Whadda you mean?" Kenneth asked. "Come on...we didn't wrestle all that much."

"But you were roommates...and you were sucking each other weren't you?" Marsha questioned.

"Well yes...when we wrestled."

"No! Wrestling has little to do with it! You guys like sucking each other don't you? Come on Kenneth tell the truth...you guys like it don't you?" Marsha challenged.

"Wrestling has everything to do with it!" Kenneth insisted.

"You're saying you guys never sucked each other without wrestling first?" Marsha asked in disbelief.

"No...I'm not saying that!" Kenneth admitted. "Mostly yes, but while we were in college it came and went...you know. In between girlfriends we sucked each other a few times...but that's all we did! Hey there's nothing wrong with that...no different than two girls licking each other. It's not like we were screwing."

"You didn't try?" Marsha quietly asked.

"Well...yeah we tried...sort of...but it hurt...and sucking felt good...so a few times we jerked or sucked each other off. Nothing serious...just buddy stuff!" Kenneth insisted.

"So you two go into the woods and suck each other off all weekend then you come home hot for David...how stupid of me to think it was because you missed me," Marsha snapped.

"Naw...naw it's not like that at all, it's really all about you," Kenneth wailed. "Being with David reminds me of when we were in college...I get charged up, excited and horny. Horny for you! Like back when we first met. I can't tell you how I've wished you were there with us. I mean it Marsha! A good physical encounter only gets a man really ready for sex. I don't know how to explain it...it's kind of like a workout or practice before a game. David is like my trainer or coach. He gets my cock in shape...hard and horny. Then it's ready for you...cause nothing or no one is sweeter or more wonderful than you and I love it when my cock is really hard and I ache for you."

"And that's why you come home horny?" Marsha asked with obvious suspicion.

"Yep! That's why I always come home horny!" Kenneth beamed, proud of his explanation.

"Take off your clothes!" Marsha ordered.

When both were undressed Marsha grabbed Kenneth's hard-on and led him to their bed. Drunk, emotionally drained and sexually overheated, the sex was frantic, brief and forgettable. Within a very few minutes both were sound asleep.

Chapter two

*M*arsha *awoke anything but at ease* with Kenneth's secret. She felt angry, betrayed and cheated. The sanctity of her marriage had repeatedly been violated right from the start and Marsha found it frightening to realize that her husband had an ongoing sexual relationship with a man…a hidden homosexual relationship that preceded her. The fact that Kenneth had been so casual about discussing it only made her more angry. Among other things, she wondered just how far they really went. She only half believed Kenneth's wrestling story and found herself wanting revenge. Marsha now regretted knowing and felt trapped inside an ugly, embarrassing secret she could not share or discuss with anyone, especially friends or family.

Kenneth on the other hand had been liberated by his confession, having bared his soul he was sexually energized and raring to go. But…Marsha was now the disinterested partner. For the first time in their married life, she felt a permanent distance between them. It was not a comfortable feeling and she made no effort to hide it, which caused Kenneth's sexual energy to quickly fade. The demands of their professions and leisure pursuits consumed most of their time and very quickly their sex life receded into its all but nonexistent state. Unsure and very frustrated Marsha managed to keep sex and Kenneth's kink out of her mind for a few weeks, until a phone call from David brought the whole issue sharply back into focus. His mother-in-law was suddenly hospitalized and his wife and children had left town to be with her. David was free for a weekend of fishing.

Ecstatic, Kenneth jumped at the chance, assuring David he would meet him at their cabin, then begged Marsha to go with him. Marsha however would not commit. Spending the weekend watching Kenneth and David grope each other was not her idea of a good time. Additionally, she was not sure she could handle the experience and saw no good reason to find out but Kenneth kept up the pressure.

Desperate to come to terms with the future of her marriage, Marsha mustered her courage and scheduled a lunch with Tina Patterson. Tina was an administrative assistant at the law firm where Marsha worked. She was cheerful, outspoken and confident, yet it was well known around the office that her husband had been busted soliciting a male prostitute in a police sting. Tina seemed to take it in stride by coming to his rescue then simply blowing the whole thing off. She did not take it seriously nor allow it to ruin her marriage. Marsha felt this was just the person she had to talk with and could only hope Tina would not turn her secret into office gossip. As soon as they finished eating Marsha poured out her troubles, while Tina smiled and comforted her.

"Sounds to me like your man is at least Bi but probably gay and hid deep in the closet. My guess is gay," Tina commented.

"So you are saying it's over?" Marsha sighed.

"Oh no, not by a long shot honey! What you gotta do is take control!" Tina advised.

"Control...what do you mean?" Marsha asked.

"You hang out with them when they are really close, like this fishing trip, and there comes an opportunity for you to take control. Do it and after that you call all the shots...you say what he can do, when and with whom...you can dictate his whole life and have him kissing your butt! Control is sweet honey...my man worships me and I like that! I like that a lot!" Tina giggled.

"How do you take control?"

Tina searched Marsha's face for a moment, "Can I speak frank and straight?" she asked.

"Please do!" Marsha pleaded.

"Okay...fuck his lover!" Tina replied matter-of-factly.

"What?" Marsha responded with shock, obviously caught by surprise.

"Look you are going on a fishing trip with just the two of them right?" Tina insisted.

"Yeah...I guess I am?" Marsha replied.

"Okay...fuck his lover and make sure he sees it. Don't fuck your husband at all. Ignore him! Focus all your attention on his lover. Suck him...fuck him...make him eat you out...make him get off and make your ole man watch the whole thing. Then when you get back home make your husband beg for it. Tell him he was bad and don't deserve it...then punish him by making him wait for a couple of days. Make sure you dress real sexy on his punishment days. It works girl, believe me! These types of men want to be controlled and they are too scared of society to live out of the closet. That's why they are only doing each other...it's also why they hide behind us. But that's cool...they are very willing to worship us...if you work it right!" Tina instructed.

"I don't know if I can pull this off?" Marsha whined.

"You better!" Tina demanded. "You say you got a good marriage otherwise, plenty money, love, compatibility, you would be a fool to let a sexual quirk ruin all that! Take control honey...and take advantage!"

"Did you screw your husband's lover?"

"Sure did...same day I found out about him," Tina replied.

"I've never cheated on my husband before..." Marsha offered.

"Cheated!" Tina snapped. "Girl, you been getting cheated on from day one, if that's what you wanna call it! Sex is weird shit...but it ain't important enough to ruin an otherwise happy life. Long as I'm in control I can hang with my Harvey's sexual need for a man," she insisted.

"And to get control you must screw his lover?" Marsha questioned again.

"Fraid so...I don't know any other way," Tina responded. "They understand sex. They understand that while men are dominant, women are their sexual superiors. Look...your fellahs hide in the woods and play pretend games because of shame and guilt. They want each other but down deep don't believe they should...or they are afraid to admit it. Either way you gotta use that to become their bitch mother...and I'll admit that's not always easy. My Harvey's more of a bi-sexual and pretty much out of the closet...but I still took control of him and his lover. I had a feeling something was going on so I came home early from work one day and caught them sucking each other right in the middle of my living room. Honey I got so mad I made Harvey stand in the corner and watch while I made his lover eat me out and I scolded both of them while he did it. I made Harvey put both hands on his head so he couldn't play with himself, then I took a condom from their grab bag of sex toys and put it on his lover, held my nose and fucked him. I had to pretend I was screwing my favorite movie star...cause that man did not turn me on at all! But I made him get off...AND I made Harvey remove the condom so he could see his lover's juice. After that I didn't fuck Harvey, let his lover touch him or let him masturbate for a week. I made him beg...I still make both of them beg and lick my feet...really. No sex without permission from mother...and they love it. A few months ago they bought me this diamond watch so I let them cruise for some occasional spice and that's how he got busted. Now I keep a tighter leash on them. But the bottom line honey is I exploit their guilt...and their juice so they know I have the measure of both of them and they kiss my ass...he-he-he! It's nice to have your ass kissed...and the only way to live with a naughty boy! Take control Marsha honey or you will go through hell. The trip's this weekend?" Tina asked.

"Uh huh," Marsha responded.

"Okay...stop by my desk tomorrow, I'll have something that'll help you get through it," Tina advised as they headed back to the office.

The next day Marsha collected three condoms and a generous amount of cocaine from Tina then the following Friday, traveled with Kenneth to the cabin in the woods that he and David jointly owned. It was a rustic cabin with only the bare essentials. Well water plumbing, a gasoline powered generator for electricity, rustic furniture, an old refrigerator, a wood burning cooking stove, a large fireplace and a small loft. Kenneth and Marsha arrived before David, she was tense and anxious so she busied herself cleaning, then decided to spend the first evening in the loft by herself. She wanted Ken and David to forget she was there and be their normal selves.

When David arrived he engaged Kenneth in a long passionate embrace then was surprised to learn that Marsha had also come on the trip. He felt her presence was intrusive and was visibly relieved to learn she had confined herself to the loft. For both men out of sight meant out of mind, so they quickly forgot about Marsha collected their fishing gear and hurried off to catch dinner.

Meanwhile Marsha studied her drug supply. Since college her drug of choice had been valium and she had plenty. She also had the cocaine Tina provided and a bottle of wine. It had been years since Marsha had done cocaine. She sniffed a little of it and in short order was buzzing on a euphoric high. She liked the coke...it calmed her nerves and gave her confidence. She sipped the wine and thought about screwing David while Kenneth watched then giggled. "Tina's right!" she announced to no one in particular, "both of these guys are wimps...naughty little boys...playing an elaborate, stupid game that robs me of a sex life. No children and no sex life...five years of marriage and no child." She accepted the fact they had not produced children, but she would no longer tolerate this ghost of Kenneth's past. It was now her duty to seize the ghost and bring it under her control. Again she giggled and drank a long toast to Tina.

Marsha was dozing when Kenneth and David returned to the cabin. The two men happily chatted and joked while cooking several large fish. They ate quickly, drank a beer then grabbed a baseball, their gloves and went outside to play catch.

At first Marsha was angry because they had not offered her dinner. She pouted for a few minutes then cheered up when she realized they had obviously forgot she was there. She climbed down from the loft, helped herself to a large serving of fish, climbed back up and comfortably settled into a spot where she could see most of the room below without being seen.

As darkness approached, Kenneth and David came back inside and settled behind a chessboard. For close to an hour they drank beer and moved chess pieces until Kenneth made a bad move that allowed David to capture his king.

"Check and mate!" David announced.

"Oh fuck!" Kenneth gasped. "I didn't mean to move that."

"Check and mate!" David repeated.

"Shit!"

"Check and mate!" David repeated again.

"Yeah...right...okay rub it in buddy...rub it in real good! You won on the board...but I'll kick your ass on the mat!" Kenneth declared.

"Is that a challenge?" David asked.

"Well it sure sounded like one...now didn't it!" Kenneth shot back.

"You mean after getting destroyed on the board...you have the balls to challenge me to the mat?" David chuckled.

"By the ancient rules. Step on the mat and I will conquer you...then proclaim victory by shoving my cock in your mouth," Kenneth boasted.

"Like hell you will! I accept your challenge! You're gonna be drinking my jiz buddy!" David responded still chuckling.

"I'll see you on the mat!" Kenneth replied in his most threatening tone.

The two men pushed the furniture against the wall and unrolled a large thick wrestling mat. Marsha was now keenly interested and shifted to get a better view. Once the mat was in place, both men undressed and covered first themselves then the others backside with mineral oil. David adjusted a timer and stood erect in his corner, while across the mat Kenneth kneeled in his corner until their preparation time expired and the bell on the timer signaled the start of the match. No holds barred, no time limit and only two rules: rule one; both wrestlers must be on the mat at all times. If any part of either wrestler leaves the mat then they must release holds, return to the center of the mat and resume the match; rule two, this is a battle to the finish for "Manhood". The victor, being the only real man, stands proud and erect, while the defeated must kneel and honor the manhood that conquered him, by taking the victorious cock into his mouth and sucking until it nourishes him or he is pushed away.

At the sound of the bell both men crouched and for a few brief moments circled each other before engaging in a powerful struggle. Marsha watched with growing excitement. She was becoming aroused by the intensity of the struggle and their naked bodies, especially the growing hard-ons. She sniffed a little cocaine then began to finger herself when David made a move that placed him squarely on top of Kenneth, who hugged him to keep his shoulders off the mat. Kenneth fought back forcing himself upright while pushing David down and gaining a brief advantage. Each man's cock was now unusually hard and frequently sliding, bumping or thrashing against the other. Their naked bodies were gleaming with oil and sweat, muscles straining, veins bulging and chests heaving as their limbs entwined in desperate struggle. Suddenly Kenneth flipped David over and landed on top of him then for a moment both men seem to rest. David lay on his stomach with Kenneth on top of him; his cock nestled in the crack of David's ass.

"Fuck him Kenny! Go ahead fuck him good!" Marsha whispered. Surprised at herself she giggled softly and continued to finger herself.

Below her the match continued for several more minutes until David missed with a take down move and Kenneth pinned him to the mat.

"ONE!" Kenneth shouted while David struggled to break the pin. "TWO! THREE! I AM THE WINNNER!" He stepped free of David and walked around the edge of the mat flexing his muscles then stopped in the center, folded his arms across his chest and thrust his hips forward.

David rose to his knees, "Tonight sir, you are the best!" he acknowledged then continued, "I beg for a rematch and I beg to salute you sir."

"Permission granted!" Kenneth snapped.

David briefly pumped Kenneth's hard cock then slid it into his mouth and sucked. Marsha sat upright and stared at them while Kenneth rolled his head and ran his fingers through David's hair. Suddenly Marsha found herself fighting an overwhelming urge to vomit. She rolled over and laid face down until the feeling passed. When she again looked at the men below Kenneth was getting off into David's mouth.

"Ahh…yeah…oue…oue…umm! Aw yeah, yeah! Remember…boy…at this point in time…I AM YOUR CONQUEROR!" Kenneth sneered.

"Yes sir… thank you sir," David replied.

Feeling woozy, Marsha rolled over and went to sleep. She awoke three times during the night and each time she checked on the men below. The first time she noticed they were sleeping in the same bed. Both naked and lying very close together. The second time she awoke Kenneth was sucking David's cock. "So wrestling has everything to do with it huh? Yeah right buddy boy! Didn't think so!" she whispered her anger building as she watched Kenneth passionately suck David to climax, then snuggle closer before going back to sleep. The third time she awoke both men were asleep. Kenneth's head lay on David's chest and his right hand rested on his thigh. Marsha glared at him and fought back the urge to tear him limb from limb. She turned over, sniffed a bit of cocaine then climbed down from the loft and used the bathroom.

Her movement caused the men to stir and to her amazement Kenneth first massaged then sleepily sucked David's cock again for a few moments before snuggling into his arms and drifting back to sleep. The cocaine was kicking in and Marsha felt better. She moved close to the bed and looked the men over. Both were about the same size but David was leaner and more muscled. She studied David's cock in hopes that it was a little bigger than Kenneth. "Any guy has got to be bigger than Kenneth!" she quietly chuckled then thought about having sex with David and prayed it would be good. Marsha really needed a lot more sex than she was getting. She loved sex and knowing that she was going to screw this man, a man other than her husband, made her hot and wet. She became angry again when she noticed Kenneth's hard-on. That was something she did not often see. "Fucking perverts...both of you...nasty boys...Tina's right! I'm gonna punish you...both of you!" Marsha muttered as she climbed back into the loft.

Chapter three

It was late in the morning when Marsha awoke; she rubbed her eyes, stretched then looked below. The men were gone and the cabin was a mess. She climbed from the loft, took a shower and ate a light breakfast. Following that she sat on the porch for over an hour sniffing cocaine and contemplating their punishment, while waiting for Kenneth and David to return. When her patience ran out, Marsha left the porch and looked carefully around.

As a child she had spent many summers on her grandparent's farm and her grandpa had taught her how to track animals. She never forgot and people were even easier. High on coke and excited by the adventure, Marsha easily tracked Kenneth and David to a secluded spot on the lake about a half-mile away. She stopped at the edge of the clearing about thirty feet from them leaned against a tree and watched.

The two men were fishing. Sitting close together, chatting, joking and playing. They drank beer and occasionally David massaged Kenneth's neck and back. Marsha was considering making a surprise move when both men stood up, took off their clothes and jumped into the lake. David quickly surfaced, climbed out of the water, spread two towels and stretched out on his back. A few minutes later Kenneth joined him, sitting close, toweling himself then David. He laughed, roughly toweled his hair then threw the towel aside and slowly slid his hands up David's legs. He hesitated briefly, looked into David's eyes then slid his hand around David's cock, squeezed it, shook it and slowly stroked up and down. David leaned forward and said something to Kenneth who quickly lowered his head and licked his best buddy's balls, then snaked his tongue all the way up David's growing hard-on until he reached the head. He paused then slowly sucked most of David manhood in and out of his mouth. Marsha grew angry as she watched her husband suck cock with obvious delight. Kenneth repositioned himself, without releasing the cock in his mouth, allowing David to take Kenneth's cock in his hand and slowly stroke it. Marsha watched intently as David only briefly put Kenneth's cock to his lips, mostly he stroked it and talked to Kenneth who was wolfing down as much cock as he could get.

Marsha had her opportunity. She stepped into the clearing and walked right upon them while each had the others' cock in their mouth. "Don't tell me…let me guess! THE FUCKING WRESTLING MATCH WAS A DRAW…RIGHT? IS THAT IT BOYS!" she shouted.

Startled, the men quickly disengaged and started to get up.

"OH NO! STAY RIGHT WHERE YOU ARE!" Marsha demanded. "Both of you lying, naughty, nasty boys…stay right there!"

"I don't have to take this shit!" David barked as he attempted to get up.

Marsha stepped forward and pushed him back down. "Do you really want Cyndi to find out just exactly what you and Kenneth do up here David?" she snapped as she grabbed a handful of his hair then pulled and twisted, "Well do you?"

"No! Ouch! Let go!" David responded.

"Then pay attention!" Marsha ordered. "From now on you will not talk back, you will do exactly what I tell you to do and you will call me Mother...do you understand?" She pulled his hair even harder, "Goddamnit David! I asked you a question! Do you understand?"

"Ouch...yes!" David pleaded.

"Yes what?" Marsha snapped.

"Yes Mother," David meekly replied.

"Jeez Marsha!" Kenneth protested.

"Shut-up! You lying shit!" Marsha demanded. "The same thing goes for you!" She released David's hair, grabbed Kenneth's ear, dug her nails in and twisted. "You too will call me Mother...do exactly what you are told and don't even think about talking back! You will pay for your lying. Both of you! Lying...nasty...little boys, playing a stupid game with each other...at the expense of my sex life. Well the game is over, it's time to settle accounts boys and I fully intend to collect! Now get your gear and head for the cabin!"

"But we..." David began.

"SHUT-UP AND DO AS YOU ARE TOLD!" Marsha shouted. "WHAT? DID YOU SAY SOMETHING?"

"I said yeah right," David mumbled.

"WHAT!" Marsha demanded.

"Uh...I mean...yes Mother," David replied.

"GET MOVING!" Marsha ordered.

Both men were stunned and knocked off balance by Marsha's surprise attack. Without time to think and no immediate options, Kenneth and David had nowhere to run and no counter attack. They had been hunted down, seized upon and captured. They knew it and quickly surrendered, offering only meager protest. Marsha allowed them to put on their shirts and boots, but not their under-shorts or pants. She also did not allow them to talk to each other as she followed, swatting at their naked behinds with a small tree branch and berating them all the way to the cabin.

Once inside the cabin Marsha ordered the men out of their boots and shirts and then made Kenneth stand with his back flush against the straight ladder that led to the loft. She gave David a roll of duct tape and ordered him to tape both of Kenneth's wrists to a rung on the ladder above his head. David liked being naked and playing a game so he took his time. Standing very close and directly in front of Kenneth he worked slowly while rubbing his cock against Kenneth's. Marsha took notice and turned up the action, "That's enough tape David...now stroke his cock...and yours too...come on...come on do it. Squeeze them together...that's it, get your hand around both of them...you like that? Good huh? Come on David pump em! Pump em hard! Yeah good boy!" Marsha praised.

When Marsha first surprised them, Kenneth had been scared and nervous. Now standing naked, his back to the ladder with his arms taped above his head, while David stood in front of him and jointly masturbated the both of them with Marsha actually cheering him on, Kenneth relaxed. He was pleased that Marsha was okay with everything and willing to play with them. He pumped his hips, loving the feel of his cock pressed against David's and sliding back and forth in his tight grip.

"Okay David that's enough now lie down on the floor," Marsha instructed. "Right there!"

David followed orders leaving Kenneth with a throbbing hard-on while Marsha positioned his head in front of Kenneth's feet. She slowly undressed then put one foot on each side of David's head and stood facing Kenneth. Marsha smiled at him and stroked his cock. "You like that Kenny? Hum? You like that feeling?" she asked.

"Yes Mother...oh yes...I like it a lot!" Kenneth cooed.

"I know you like it Kenneth because this is my cock!" Marsha snapped. "I married it and that makes it MY COCK...and just for the record...your busy little mouth is mine too! Did you hear that David?" she demanded.

"Yes Mother," David replied, his eyes fixed on Marsha's crotch.

"Both this cock and this mouth you have been using and like so much belongs to me David," Marsha sternly advised. "And," she continued, "since you seem to like these so much...let's see how you like my pussy." She quickly lowered herself, placed one knee on each side of David's head and guided her pussy to his mouth. He hesitated for a moment then slowly began flicking his tongue across her clit. "Come on eat me you nasty bastard...eat me!" Marsha demanded, then leaned back and looked at Kenneth. He began to lose his hard-on when David started licking Marsha and she was pleased. She took Kenneth's cock in her hand again and slowly stroked it. "You lied to me Kenneth..." she taunted, "you lied...now David is licking ME...and he likes it! Don't you David?"

"Uh-huh..." David grunted, he really was liking it; Marsha was wet, sweet and moving with a good rhythm.

"Oh yeah David...you like it!" Marsha snapped. "You nasty, lying two timer...you like it and you like lying to Cyndi about it. You like Kenneth's mouth on your cock and you like lying about that too! Don't you? Tell the truth David! You are an immoral liar and you like it don't you?" she demanded.

"Yes Mother...yes...I like it!" David responded.

"Lick me you pig! Look at him Kenneth!" Marsha demanded. "Look at his cock...its hard Kenneth...real hard...bet you would like to suck it while David licks me wouldn't you?" she questioned.

Kenneth stared at David's hard-on and in spite of himself grew hard again. "Oh gosh Mother! Please...please let me suck him," he begged.

Marsha said nothing but continued to slowly pump Kenneth with her hand and ride her pussy against David's tongue. David had really gotten into it; he eagerly licked and sucked Marsha with obvious relish. After a few moments Marsha leaned over to her right, picked up her blouse and plucked a condom from the pocket. She put the condom into David's hand and ordered him to put it on.

"Uh...ah...now I don't know about..." David began in an attempt to protest.

"PUT IT ON GODDAMNIT!" Marsha demanded. "WHAT DID I TELL YOU ABOUT BACK TALK? PUT IT ON! NOW!"

"Uh...Marsha...uh..." Kenneth whined.

Marsha yanked his cock, "Shut-up Kenneth! Don't say a fucking word! You lied to me...right to my face Kenneth. You naughty, dirty, son-of-a-bitch...you lied to me! Now your suck buddy is going to fuck your wife...and you are going to watch. Look at him Kenneth! Look at your best buddy...look at him stroke his cock. Yeah...that's right...David...get it nice and hard for Mother."

Once David had the condom in place Marsha ordered him to lie back and grab Kenneth's ankles. She scooted backwards until David's cock was between her legs then set up, spread her legs and rubbed her most intimate flesh against David's aching hard-on, all while focused on Kenneth. "Oue...look Kenny...David's really hard...see...he must really want to fuck me! Do you think he wants to fuck me?" Marsha questioned. "His cock is bigger than yours Kenny; do you think I can get all of it into my pussy? Hum? Well let's just see." She rose slightly and slid David's cock into her.

Kenneth stared opened mouth but said nothing while his rigid cock throbbed in front of him. David tightly gripped Kenneth's ankles and pumped his hips in an effort to penetrate deeper, but Marsha teased him, taking very little of his cock but pumping hard and fast then slowing to an almost stop, before slowly sliding him in deep then out.

"Does it look good to you Kenneth? Do you like watching this? Do you like seeing David's cock in my pussy? DO YOU?" Marsha demanded.

"No Mother," Kenneth whimpered.

"Then why is your cock hard Kenneth?" Marsha snapped. "You're a liar! A sorry liar! You like something about this picture don't you? You like seeing his cock hard and you want it in your mouth don't you? You're a cocksucker Kenneth...and you even lie to yourself about that...don't you?" she demanded.

"Y...yes...yes Mother," Kenneth responded as tears trickled down his face.

"You're a cocksucker Kenneth!" Marsha snapped. "Say it goddamnit! Let me hear you tell the fucking truth. SAY IT!" she demanded.

"I'm a cocksucker!" Kenneth blurted out. "I love sucking David's cock..."

"Right this instant you would choose his cock over my pussy wouldn't you?" Marsha sharply questioned. "Wouldn't you godddamit!"

"Ye...yes Mother...I would," Kenneth loudly responded while sobbing and sniffing.

Marsha glared at Kenneth then placed both hands on David's chest and worked all of him inside her. She briefly rode up and down still glaring at Kenneth before turning her attention to the man and cock Kenneth so desired. "David? Do you want to fuck me or not?" she snapped.

"Uh...yes mother," David replied.

"YES MOTHER WHAT?" Marsha demanded.

"Uh...yes Mother I want to fuck you," David responded with enthusiasm.

"Then get on top and act like it goddamnit! Come on David...fuck your buddy's wife...right in front of his face!" Marsha ordered. "WELL..."

David was overwhelmed by Marsha's domination. He was thrilled and powerless, both her tight, hot snatch and the helpless presence of Kenneth excited him pass any point of return. He released Kenneth's ankles, grabbed Marsha, rolled over, settled between her legs then pushed into her.

"Watch us Kenneth!" Marsha called out. "Watch us fuck!" She raised her legs and met David's every thrust, desperately wanting an exciting climax but David proved to be no better a lover than Kenneth. To Marsha's great disappointment he soon shot his load into the condom. She immediately pushed him over and slid off being careful to keep the condom in place.

As she stood up David reached for his still pulsing cock. "Don't you dare touch it David!" she snapped then reached out and stroked Kenneth's cock. "You want to fuck Mother now baby...hum?" she teased.

"Yes...oh yes Mother...YES!" Kenneth begged, eager for her forgiveness and eager for relief from his aching hard-on.

Marsha ran her tongue across Kenneth's lips and stroked his cock with her hand pleased that he was hard. "Well...you're not going to!" she replied then cut the tape that bound Kenneth's hands to the ladder, "Get that condom off David and dispose of it...NOW!"

Kenneth obeyed, eagerly squeezing and pumping David's cock as he removed the condom. He briefly stared at David's load then tossed the condom into the fireplace.

Marsha put on her clothes but did not allow the men to dress. She was truly surprised at herself and quietly amazed at the ease of her take over and the speed at which the men accepted her role and obeyed orders without question or protest. She ordered them to prepare lunch then thoroughly clean the cabin from top to bottom, while she sniffed tiny bits of cocaine and closely watched them. She rewarded good work with beer and when they occasionally brushed against each other while cleaning she made them stop what they were doing. After berating them she would allow them to briefly fondle each other until they were both hard. She wanted their cocks hard and their balls heavy...and for the remainder of this trip she would keep them that way.

Cleaning the cabin to Marsha's satisfaction took the rest of the day. It was evening when David and Kenneth finished, prepared dinner then cleaned up afterwards. Marsha was pleased and allowed them two beers each and a few moments to fondle each other...but not get off.

Finally in an ultimate test of her power, Marsha undressed, sat on the table, ordered the men to the floor then placed one foot to each man's lips. "Suck my toes nasty boys...suck em good...real good," she ordered. Much to her surprise, without any hesitation both men eagerly sucked her toes and licked her feet.

High on cocaine and enjoying her power Marsha liked being the bitch mother but was slightly annoyed by one nagging fact. Throughout her entire sex life she always had the feeling that something just wasn't there. She did not know what that something was, just that it wasn't there. Now with two male slaves at her disposal she set out to find that missing something. Repositioning herself to the bed, she ordered the men back to work on her feet and promised if either of them came, he would spend the night taped to the ladder while the other would enjoy the night in bed with her.

After several moments, she turned onto her stomach and ordered them to slowly kiss her entire body, from the soles of her feet up to her neck. They responded enthusiastically and for several long moments slowly kissed, nibbled and tongue massaged the entire backside of Marsha's naked body. Delighted with their performance, she relaxed and completely enjoyed the experience. She closed her eyes in pleasure when David's wet tongue pushed deep into the crack of her ass then slid up and down. Marsha turned over and let them completely lick the front side of her, holding each man's head in her hand while they slowly licked and sucked her tits. She was boiling hot when their tongues slid up and down her inner thighs then approached her crotch. She soared and relished her power as each man took long turns at licking and sucking her cunt. Marsha enjoyed her climax, but that missing something was still missing. For a moment she considered screwing both of them in rapid succession but deep inside knew that whatever that certain missing something was neither Kenneth nor David could deliver it. She then pondered allowing them to briefly suck each other but decided against that too and finally ordered them to follow her to the shower. David and Kenneth gently washed then dried Marsha. They massaged her body with lotion then wrapped her in a robe.

It was now getting late, the following day was Sunday and they would leave for home around noon so both David and Kenneth begged Marsha for permission to wrestle one last time. At first she refused but granted permission for them to continue begging. Still high on cocaine and for the moment, ruling Queen of an all-male colony, Marsha thoroughly enjoyed seeing Kenneth and David grovel and beg before her.

"So you boys want to wrestle...hum?" she teased.

"Yes...please Mother...please!" the men begged.

"Wrestling is an honorable sport...you are not honorable boys...you are nasty little liars...and cocksuckers...both of you! If you really want to wrestle then you must confess the true depths of your feelings for each other and become real men by doing so. Are you prepared to do that?" Marsha demanded.

"Yes Mother," they replied in unison.

"Very well..." Marsha sighed. "Stand before me. Both of you...now hug each other tightly."

Kenneth and David pressed their naked bodies together and held tightly to each other.

"Look into each other's eyes," Marsha continued. "Look deep...feel his body...feel his cock and tell the truth with your eyes. Now kiss!"

"Uh...we don't kiss Mother," David offered.

"WHAT DID I JUST TELL YOU TO DO?" Marsha snapped. "DON'T EVER TELL ME WHAT YOU DON'T DO! KISS HIM GODDAMNIT! KISS HIM DEEP AND NASTY! DO IT! NOW!" she shrieked.

Kenneth's lips met David's with a quick peck. Then another longer peck that lingered and slowly developed into a long wet kiss that resulted in both men holding tightly to each other while grinding their hips.

"Okay...you can wrestle!" Marsha snorted, disgusted with their enthusiastic kiss.

Kenneth and David quickly spread the wrestling mat, oiled each other, set the timer and began their mental preparation while Marsha watched with little interest. After the bell rang the match began and for over ten minutes the two men grabbed, twisted, struggled, strained and tried to get the better of the other.

When she grew bored Marsha went to the sink and filled a large bowl with cold water. She then stepped to the edge of the mat, threw the water on the men and announced, "I declare this match a draw!"

Startled, the men sprang apart, "What! No!" they protested.

"The match is a draw and that's final!" Marsha insisted. "David, you got ninety seconds to get in and out of the shower...and you Kenneth, clean up that mat! NOW! GET A MOVE ON! BOTH OF YOU!" she ordered.

David headed to the shower while Kenneth wiped the oil and sweat from the mat. In short order David stepped from the shower.

"Kenneth ninety seconds and don't you dare play with your cock. David, put that mat away," she instructed. When Kenneth stepped from the shower, Marsha ordered the men to bed and was amused when they climbed into the same bed and lay close together.

She changed into a long flannel bodysuit and climbed into the same bed, positioning herself between the two naked men. She made them lay on their backs, then reached out and took a cock in each hand. She stroked them until they were hard then released them. After several minutes she stroked them hard again, feeling their balls and smiling as she knew each man was aching for relief. After a time she allowed them to drift off to sleep, but she stayed awake for a short while watching their cocks, teasing and keeping them hard even while they slept. Suddenly Kenneth's cock began to jerk as though it were going to cum. Marsha slapped it hard and Kenneth awoke, his balls were aching and his cock was quickly going soft.

"What...oh...umh...what?" he mumbled.

"Go to sleep baby... go back to sleep...it was just a bad dream," Marsha whispered then chuckled as she gently gripped Kenneth and stroked him hard yet again.

Marsha finally went to sleep and awoke early Sunday morning with both men still sleeping and snuggled against her. She felt for their cocks and finding them almost hard pleased her greatly. For a time she looked at them, one on each side. Two men of her very own. "Hum...two little nasty boys," she whispered. Still, possessing two obedient males conjured up many possibilities. She pondered for a few moments then concluded with the honest thought that since neither of them satisfied nor really excited her, there was little reason to consider any sexual possibilities. Disappointed, she gripped their cocks, yanked hard and shouted, "HIT THE FUCKING FLOOR GENTLEMEN...AND FIX MY BREAKFAST!"

Both men jumped out of bed and stumbled around, going to the bathroom, stretching, yawning and coming to life. They prepared breakfast, ate, and cleaned up the dishes. Marsha then allowed them to play a game of chess on the front porch while she sniffed cocaine and swayed in the porch swing. When the chess game was over, Marsha closely supervised as Kenneth and David briefly fondled each other, dressed, then closed up the cabin.

When they were prepared to leave all three of them were standing next to their cars in front of the cabin. Marsha massaged David's cock hard yet again then took him into her arms. "You have been a good boy and I am going to keep your dirty little secret. In fact I'm going to invite you and Cyndi to visit. I'll plan lots of activity for Cyndi and the kids, so you and Kenneth will have plenty of time alone. Would you like that?" she asked.

"Yes Mother...thank you," David replied.

"You're welcome David! Remember...obey your Mother and good things will happen. Disobey and I will destroy you! Understand?"

"Yes Mother," David responded.

"Good boy! Now kiss me!" Marsha ordered.

David touched his lips to Marsha and she overwhelmed him, pushing her tongue deep into his mouth and sucking his lips with hers. She pulled his hair and forced him back against his car, grinding her crotch against him and sucking his tongue. David gasped then returned the pleasure, giving as much back as he possibly could. For a moment he lost himself to Marsha, his cock hard as nails and balls aching for relief.

Kenneth stood close by and watched with very mixed emotions. It was extremely uncomfortable to see his wife locked in a passionate embrace with another man and it was worse to have watched her fuck him. Kenneth was torn because he loved David and would have shared Marsha if David had insisted. But, Marsha had taken charge and given herself to David while punishing both of them. She had forced him and David look at their relationship in a more honest way and she also made him openly confess his need and desire for this man. Marsha was now Mother and Kenneth was developing a genuine fear of her. He shuffled his feet and grunted throughout Marsha and David's long hot kiss.

Finally Marsha broke off the kiss. She placed her hands against David's shoulders, pushed her leg inside his, positioned her crotch against his hard-on and dry fucked him. "Do you love me David?" she cooed. "Do you love Mother?"

"Oh yes! Yes! I love you Mother...I really do...I really love you!" David cried out as he attempted to kiss Marsha again but she stepped away.

"Okay Kenneth! Your turn!" she snapped.

"Huh? What?" Kenneth questioned.

"Say good-bye stupid!" Marsha ordered. "Hug him...feel his cock...kiss him. You know you want to...so do it! NOW KENNETH!"

David reached out and pulled Kenneth into his arms. Kenneth's hand immediately felt for and found David's cock. It was rock hard...causing Kenneth to feel faint and weak as he melted into David's embrace. With one hand David cupped Kenneth's chin and with the other he massaged his buddy's ass as their lips made contact. Kenneth's arms slid around David's shoulders and neck as their kiss grew wet, intense and extremely passionate...igniting their long simmering spark into a flickering flame.

Both were panting, sweating, incredibly hard and desperately wanting more when Marsha sang out, "Okay enough guys...save something for next time. Okay enough already...I SAID ENOUGH ALREADY! GODDAMNIT! Good-bye David!" she snapped.

The two men slowly separated looking deep into each other's eyes, before Kenneth quickly turned away, not wanting to see his buddy leave.

"Good-bye Mother. So long buddy...I love you guys!" David gushed then hopped into his BMW and drove away, cock hard and balls aching.

Marsha and Kenneth climbed into their Jeep and headed for home. A long drive during which Marsha constantly berated Kenneth and reminded him that David had licked and fucked her. Occasionally she would massage his cock until he was hard and he would beg her to stop. Kenneth had been aroused almost constantly for over twenty-four hours without getting off and his hard-ons now produced sharp pains in his balls. He wanted to cum, he had to cum but if that wasn't going to happen then he didn't want to be touched at all. Marsha knew Kenneth was in agony, she was very pleased with that and continued to insure his discomfort for the rest of that day.

Over the following three days Marsha dressed very provocatively and relentlessly berated or taunted Kenneth, trying to keep him hard but not letting him cum. In spite of her warnings however, Kenneth furiously masturbated in a locked bathroom at work his first morning back on the job. To his dismay, he came with great relief and great pain. His balls never hurt so bad...it was precisely what Mother had told him would happen if he masturbated. He washed up and returned to his desk with considerable lingering physical discomfort and an uneasy feeling of guilt for having disobeyed Mother, a lady for whom he now had even more respect...and fear.

Late that following Thursday evening Marsha again stroked Kenneth hard. This time she undressed, climbed onto the bed and said, "Come on Kenneth. Come fuck Mother...come on baby!" Kenneth quickly climbed on top of her and fucked hard. In but a few quick moments, he turned red as the veins bulged in his neck and cum exploded from his aching hard-on. He collapsed and Marsha held him in her arms for almost two hours before he again got hard. She wanted a long slow fuck but allowed Kenneth to fuck her rapidly again before cumming quickly and collapsing. Marsha smiled, he wasn't much in bed but he was hers and now totally under her control. She stroked his hair, eased him off her and went to sleep. To his surprise and delight the next morning, Marsha allowed Kenneth to repeat his performance of the night before. He came with great joy and true relief from the aching in his genitals. That very same evening right after work, Kenneth bought twelve very expensive red roses then hurried home to Mother.

Chapter four

*B*y *Saturday Kenneth had transformed* into a completely obedient servant. He rose early and happily prepared then served Marsha breakfast in bed. After she finished eating, he ate in the kitchen, cleaned up the dishes, vacuumed then carpets, done the laundry and cleaned the bathrooms while Marsha lazily read the morning newspaper. Although he wasn't really ready to admit it, Kenneth liked his subservient role. He smiled while cleaning the remainder of the house, then took it upon himself to prepare a hot bubble bath for Marsha.

Very pleased with Kenneth's performance Marsha slipped into the pleasant water. She felt great and Kenneth was the perfect bath attendant. Wearing only a towel wrap as Mother had ordered, he poured champagne put on the right music and lit fragrance candles. Marsha floated in hot soapy bliss for several long moments then ordered Kenneth to slowly wash her entire body with lots of soap. Becoming giddy from the champagne, she ordered Kenneth to dress and rush out for grapes, green grapes. In less than fifteen minutes, Kenneth returned to the tub with green grapes and cheese in hand, but Marsha was not pleased. He had taken too long and her bath water had cooled. Kenneth quickly turned on the hot water, changed back into his towel wrap, poured more champagne then fed Marsha grapes and cheese. He washed her hair as instructed then stood by until she finally stood up so he could rinse and dry her. When she stepped from the tub, Kenneth combed and blow-dried her hair, then meekly followed mother to the bedroom.

For close to an hour Marsha lay naked on her bed totally relaxed while Kenneth slowly massaged her. She was pleased with the outcome of her adventure although her victory seemed somewhat bittersweet. Her marital relationship had changed forever. Marsha now had little respect for Kenneth and while it was nice to have an obedient wimp it did little for her deep longings for a man, a real man. She sighed aloud then chuckled. True Kenneth wasn't much…but now he was completely and totally hers. His needs and wishes were completely unimportant…fulfilling Mother's commands were now Kenneth's first priority.

For a few moments, Marsha studied Kenneth and questioned her new role before assuring herself it was more than a satisfactory substitute for the true longings within her soul. That unfulfilled longing she could not describe, identify or really understand anyway. She turned over and spread her legs then grabbed Kenneth by the hair, guided his mouth to the correct spot and kept him there until she climaxed. A short time later Marsha allowed Kenneth to penetrate her, expecting and getting very little from his predictably unexciting and woefully short performance.

The following Monday Marsha treated Tina to a very expensive lunch. She beamed with pride while sharing all the details of the weekend at the cabin with her two men and Kenneth's subsequent development. Tina was impressed and absolutely delighted. She offered a toast to Marsha from one bitch-mother to another as they laughed, chatted and made arrangements for Marsha to purchase two grams of cocaine.

Later that evening Marsha watched Kenneth tidy up the kitchen, then ordered him to bed. She really wasn't sexually aroused but was hoping frequent sex would make Kenneth a better lover. She teased him hard, sat astride him, slowly slid his cock into her, briefly rode up and down then ordered Kenneth to take charge and do it the way he liked it best. Kenneth gently pushed Marsha onto her back, climbed on top of her and delivered his usual quickie. Afterwards he collapsed then drifted into contented sleep. Marsha lightly stroked Kenneth's hair then turned over and closed her eyes trying to escape the thought that her victory seemed hollow at best.

The demands of the business week usually left little time for extensive interaction between the Weber's. By late Wednesday evening after a full day of work, a ninety-minute seminar and several minutes of networking and informal chatting afterwards, Marsha was exhausted. When she arrived at home she was thinking only of a hot bath, but found Kenneth sitting at the dining room table drinking heavily. His eyes were puffy and red and he did not look in her direction until she spoke. "Kenneth! What's the matter?"

"David can't go fishing anymore!" he blurted out.

"What...did you just talk to him?" Marsha questioned.

"Yeah...little while ago."

"What exactly did he say?" Marsha inquired.

"He told Cyndi that he went fishing while she was away and she got really pissed. He said something about his being away all weekend and not even calling to see how her sick mother was..." Kenneth blew his nose, wiped his eyes then continued. "Anyway he promised her he would never go fishing again...and she's making him sell his share of the cabin to prove it."

"My God! How much about the weekend did he tell her?" Marsha questioned.

"I dunno...everything I guess."

Marsha picked up the phone and dialed David's house but there was no answer. Kenneth continued to wipe his nose and drink.

"This means I'll never see him again! Never..." he whimpered.

"Of course you will, now stop overreacting!" Marsha snapped. She capped the bottle of liquor, put it back in the cabinet and ordered Kenneth into the shower.

Following a light dinner Marsha briefly looked at the mail then called David's number again, and again there was no answer. "Kenneth? Does David and Cyndi have caller ID?" she called out.

"Uh yeah...probably," Kenneth replied.

"Hum...well we'll give them a few days...then see how things stand," Marsha concluded.

"I promised David I would send a check for his share of the cabin within the week," Kenneth advised.

"How much is that?" Marsha asked.

"Uh...we agreed on eight thousand dollars," Kenneth responded.

"Kenneth!" Marsha shrieked.

"I'm sorry Mother...I was over a barrel!" Kenneth whined. "She was gonna leave him...he had to tell her something...and I know the cabin gotta be worth more than sixteen thousand...that's about what we paid for it...and..."

"Okay...settle down honey, I understand!" Marsha assured. "Just don't mail that check until the absolute last minute...and don't be surprised if David changes his mind about selling. Now prepare my bath then go to bed," she ordered.

Kenneth did as he was told but without any enthusiasm. A gloomy funk now possessed him and grew worse when David emailed an inquiry as to the whereabouts of the check, which Kenneth immediately mailed.

By the time the "Quit Claim Deed" arrived Marsha was perplexed, frustrated and fed up with Kenneth's funk. This document meant David had cashed the check and Kenneth was now the sole owner of the cabin in the woods. The sight of the Quit Claim Deed brought tears to Kenneth's eyes. He fought to hold them back but lost the battle, breaking down and weeping openly and loudly for several moments. Marsha let him cry it out then consoled and comforted him. It was sad...sad for both of them. But Marsha had little time for sad and Kenneth's funk had already lasted too long. She wanted to snap him out of it and breathe some zest back into their lives...but went to bed searching for alternatives to what she knew to be the real answer.

Two more days of Kenneth's dark gloomy funk was all that Marsha could stand. She ordered him to pour drinks then sit and relax. After the second drink Marsha got right to the point. "Kenneth, you need a new playmate!" she announced.

"What?" Kenneth questioned in surprise.

"Look the only way you are going to get over David is to find a new playmate and that's what you are going to do," Marsha instructed.

"Jeez...I dunno..." Kenneth whined. "I wouldn't wanna wrestle with any guy other than David."

"Kenneth!" Marsha snapped. "Right now David is out of the picture and you need to wrestle don't you?"

"Yes Mother," Kenneth admitted.

"And you need to lose the match...right?"

"I...ah...uh..." Kenneth stammered.

"You don't really need to wrestle, you need a cock to play with...don't you Kenneth?" Marsha sharply questioned.

"I need both Mother...I really do..."

"Then you must find a new playmate honey," Marsha advised.

"Jeez...I dunno...I'm not sure...I ah..." Kenneth replied in a struggle for words.

"Kenneth, I been closely watching you lately," Marsha responded. "You stare at men's crotches a lot. I'm sure some of them must stare back...and there are some you like...right?" she probed.

"Uh...yeah sure."

"Okay then! Select one and feel him out," Marsha advised, "do dinner or something. I want you to start thinking about this right now Kenneth. I want you to find yourself a playmate. Once you have picked him out

I will have the final say...but for now I am giving you to the opportunity to pick him. Do you understand?" she questioned.

"Well...yeah...I guess," Kenneth replied.

"No! Not guess Kenneth!" Marsha snapped. "You're not trying to find the impossible...just one guy that can pass my scrutiny and provide what you need. Have you got that?" she demanded with growing impatience.

"Uh...yeah. Yes Mother...yes I do!" Kenneth responded. Marsha's words were beginning to sink in and Kenneth was becoming absorbed with the thought of fondling a strange new man. The more he thought about it the more convinced he became of Marsha's wisdom and the rightness of her decision. His mood brightened considerably and Marsha seized the opportunity, taunting Kenneth's hunger for man meat while getting him very hard and horny. To her delight and surprise he pushed her down and licked her to climax while furiously masturbating.

Kenneth went to sleep that night excited by thoughts of finding a new wrestling buddy and Marsha drifted off to sleep pleased that her strategy had worked. She didn't really expect Kenneth would actually find a new playmate but it was important to direct his focus away from David and for now fantasizing about other men was the only way. Marsha was confident that in time she would wean Kenneth of his fantasies and perversion. But, much to her complete amazement Kenneth took his assignment seriously. Within only a few days he had invited a business consultant and his wife out to dinner with him and Marsha. Kenneth was glowing with excitement. This was the perfect guy, slightly older, about the same physical size and they even shared a deep passion for wrestling and fishing. Not to mention the many racy conversations they had shared. Marsha was skeptical but had no real reason to refuse so she went out to dinner with John and Kathy Wilcox.

The four adults enjoyed a good meal and each others company, while their conversation grew increasingly erotic and openly flirtatious. By the time after dinner drinks were served, Marsha overwhelming approved of John and Kathy and though it had not been said, she was now somewhat willing to let Kenneth and herself sexually experiment with either or both of them. However, judging from John's conversation Marsha did not think he shared Kenneth's desire for male contact. She wanted to go slow but Kenneth insisted on spelling out the rules of Ancient Greco Wrestling. When he finished John asked him to repeat them which Kenneth did, prompting John and Kathy to storm out of the restaurant insulted, disgusted and angry. Kenneth was crestfallen, but four days later bounced right back with another "perfect guy". Reluctantly, Marsha went to dinner with Brian and Georgia Thompson. Brian, an office machine repairman was physically bigger than Kenneth and to Marsha both Brian and Georgia seemed course and objectionable. As soon as dinner was over, Kenneth eagerly explained the rules of Ancient Greco Wrestling, after which Brian threatened to whip his ass then, with Georgia in tow, abruptly left the restaurant without paying their bill.

Marsha was fed up, later that evening she ordered Kenneth to massage her feet. "Kenneth I think you are going about this boy thing the wrong way," she advised.

"I don't know how to do it any better," Kenneth replied.

"Well...honey, what's with this wrestling?" Marsha questioned. "You know that's just a front for what you really want."

"No! No it's not really..." Kenneth protested. "I mean...ah sure...ah...I like going down on a guy...and probably would if we didn't wrestle...but Ancient Greco is in my blood...I need it just as bad," he explained.

"Then maybe you should explain the rules up front, before we get embarrassed again in another restaurant," Marsha suggested.

"God...I really miss David," Kenneth whimpered as tears began to trickle down his face.

To change the mood, Marsha ordered Kenneth to stand naked before a full-length mirror and fondle himself. Already annoyed, she became fully agitated when Kenneth failed to produce a hard-on. Marsha picked up a wide leather belt and slapped it hard against Kenneth's ass then berated him for being a naughty boy. To her pleasant surprise Kenneth began masturbating furiously. She ordered him closer to the mirror then slapped his ass with the belt again and again, leaving a glowing red welt. Kenneth pumped his cock and loudly wailed until the sting of the leather across his burning ass caused his cum to explode onto the mirror.

Marsha was breathing hard, perspiring and very excited. "Get down on your fucking knees right now boy!" she demanded.

"Yes mother!" Kenneth replied then dropped to his knees.

"Lick it off...all of it! Lick every fucking drop of your goddamn filthy cum off my mirror...NOW!" she ordered.

Kenneth quickly obeyed. His head was swimming...his emotions swirled while his burning ass glowed red. Mother stood over him snapping the leather belt in her hand while he meekly licked his own cum from the mirror.

With cum still on his lips and gathered on the head of his cock, Marsha slipped the belt around Kenneth's neck and lead him to the bed like a dog. She sat on the edge of the bed and made him eat her while berating him. "Lick me good...just like you were sucking a cock you nasty shit...freaky little nasty boy! Yeah put your tongue right there...ah yeah...eat me damn you. You fucking dirty little cocksucker...you would rather be sucking a big hard cock wouldn't you? You're a nasty perverted bastard Kenneth Weber! Eat me goddamnit! Eat me! Faster...come on little boy...come on...uh huh...come on."

In spite of being highly aroused Marsha soon became frustrated. She had approached climax three times, yet each time she could not quite reach it. She ordered Kenneth to his feet, hoping to see a hard-on but was disappointed. Her frustration only increased when no amount of fondling by either of them could produce the much-desired woody. She ordered Kenneth to wash the mirror, take a shower then go to bed while she attempted to still the need within her body by slowly fingering herself until she fell asleep.

Kenneth was greatly energized by his ass whipping. He now understood that there could only be one Mother, so he changed his strategy and invited a single guy out to dinner. Jason McKinsky was a real jock that worked at the tennis club. Jason was younger, bigger and stronger than Kenneth. He had been on the wrestling team in high school and college, knew the rules of Ancient Greco Wrestling and could become a real buddy.

Marsha was not impressed. She went to dinner expecting nothing more than a good meal and was not disappointed. Jason McKinsky was boorish, vain and very conceited. Marsha considered Jason completely obnoxious and tried her best to ignore him, in spite of the fact he ogled her throughout dinner, while Kenneth ogled him. After dinner Jason agreed to wrestle Kenneth by the Ancient Greco rules, with one exception. That exception being the winner gets Marsha instead of a blowjob from the loser. Marsha was outraged! The very idea that she was suggested as the prize in a lowbrow wrestling match infuriated her. She was shocked however to find Kenneth more outraged than her. Kenneth was absolutely unyielding about the rules. None could be altered, excepted or broken and he was completely livid at the suggestion. But Jason insisted…and on that night it was Marsha and Kenneth who left the restaurant indignant.

Feeling down-spirited Kenneth began easing back into his funk. His best efforts had come up short and his confidence was now nonexistent. Marsha acted quickly by confiding in Tina then accepting an invitation to dinner with her and her husband. Tina's husband was bisexual so there was at least common ground. Kenneth was delighted with the news but the dinner was awkward and uncomfortable. The truth was, both men were passive and resented the lack of aggression in the other. Harvey thought wrestling was common and barbaric and he certainly had no intention of ever doing such a thing, while Kenneth quickly decided Harvey was a fag. Kenneth did not like fags or queers. His only interest was in men...real men. The evening ended quietly and over the next couple of weeks, little mention was made of sex in the Weber house.

Marsha was not disappointed with Kenneth's failure to produce a playmate. It played right into her plan to rid him of any desire for a man. She consciously allowed sex to recede deep into the background of their lives, hoping to starve Kenneth and make him beg for sex, but he seemed quite content without any.

By late Saturday evening of the third sexless week Marsha was restless and on edge. Her strategy for dealing with Kenneth had left her own desires woefully unattended. She wanted sex but feared that at this point if she went after Kenneth aggressively it would only awaken the very desire she was attempting to bury. After channel surfing for a while Marsha snapped off the television and looked at Kenneth who was absorbed in a magazine. The same magazine he had been absorbed in for the last two days. "What are you reading?" she asked.

"Uh... just a magazine."

"What kind of magazine? Let me see it," she demanded.

"It's no big deal...really Mother," Kenneth pleaded.

"Kenneth! Give me the magazine!" Marsha ordered. Kenneth promptly handed over his now treasured copy of "The Tri-State Swingers Directory". Marsha briefly looked through the magazine containing pictures and ads with contact information of people looking for various sexual encounters. "Where did you get this?" she asked.

"Uh...at the adult shop...in that strip mall up the street. I was coming home after work and I looked over and saw the store...and it hit me...just like the man says, hell I been looking for love in all the wrong places," Kenneth beamed.

Marsha took a closer look at the magazine then chuckled. The chuckle was really the releasing of her quiet frustration. This magazine meant her strategy was not working as she had hoped. Kenneth was still fantasizing about and actively seeking a new male play buddy. Marsha regretted the day she first discovered the truth, she now felt weary and beleaguered. It seemed an unfair burden that required a lot of work and vigilance to keep under control. She looked at Kenneth and dearly wished she could slap his perverted desires right out of him, but knowing that wasn't possible she decided to punish him for buying such a book without her permission.

Marsha made Kenneth strip and bend over with his arms extended to the edge of the sofa. She slowly paced around him in silence for several moments then undressed and picked up her wide leather belt. The last time she had only teased him with the belt but this time he would truly feel it. She slapped the leather hard across Kenneth's ass and was delighted when he jerked and cried out in pain. She delivered another powerful slap and felt a wonderful sense of power, so she slapped Kenneth's ass again and again with growing excitement.

Kenneth felt as though his entire body was on fire. The pain was horrible yet delicious. His balls were contracting, he was drooling, his nose dripped and water ran from his eyes when Marsha ordered him to his knees. She made him eat her while she reclined on the sofa, berating and exciting him with graphic descriptions of men in heat.

It was too late when Marsha discovered that while Kenneth was doing his level best on her, he was also masturbating. It had been weeks and she dearly wanted his hard cock inside her but he had already shot his load on the sofa and rug. Marsha was sorely disappointed and genuinely pissed off. She first threatened to give Kenneth more lashes but instead ordered him to scrub the sofa and rug, prepare her bath then go to bed. Feeling drained and unfulfilled, Marsha lingered in the bath for some time then went to sleep that night wondering if her marriage would last.

Over the next two weeks, Marsha watched with quiet amusement as Kenneth busied himself analyzing various ads in The Tri-State Swingers Directory. For one reason or another Kenneth rejected each selected ad, nobody really fit what he was looking for. With Marsha's approval he exchanged messages with a few of the ads and found a few gay guys, a wife-swapper and a couple guys who were really looking for another guy to do their wife, but no one looking for a wrestling buddy. Finally he asked Marsha for permission to submit his own ad.

In honest truth Marsha was now fed up with Kenneth. She had no respect for him, he did nothing for her sexually, their marriage vows were a joke and there were no illusions left. She gave her permission only with the faint hope that he may turn up someone sexually interesting to her. Kenneth immediately began writing his ad, making such a production about it, Marsha decided to supervise.

"Now...first...hum..." Kenneth pondered.

"Well if you are going to advertise then ask for the best...your perfect guy," Marsha suggested.

"Yeah...you're right!" Kenneth agreed.

"Just describe David and be done with it," Marsha advised.

"No! I mean...I don't want an imitation David!" Kenneth responded. "There's only one David...I want to advertise for my fantasy man."

"Really? Who is your fantasy man?"

"I dunno know..." Kenneth replied. "Never actually thought about it but I know what I like."

"Okay start from there, write down all the things you would like this man to be or have or do," Marsha instructed.

"Okay...let's see...ah...he should be about my physical size for wrestling and older. Yeah at least ten years older than me,"

"Ten years older? Why?" Marsha questioned.

"Hell...wisdom and strength!" Kenneth proudly announced then continued. "The most potent essence on earth comes only from the most fierce, brave, weathered and seasoned warrior! A veteran who's been through it...you know what I mean? Been through it and back several times...and still strong. I would pay to drink his essence."

"Kenneth you disgust me," Marsha hissed.

"I'm sorry Mother...please forgive...please?" Kenneth begged.

"Never mind...go on with your ad," Marsha sighed.

"Uh...yeah okay. A slim guy in his forties must like to fish, wrestle nude and be serviced orally. How's that?"

"Okay...I guess," Marsha responded with little enthusiasm.

"No! I mean...I'm gonna do it over," Kenneth pleaded. Several minutes later he read his new version. "Okay...thirty something white couple, he is 5'9", 174, she is 5'6", 127, seeking same sized forty something, straight, single or divorced black male. Veteran a plus. Must like to fish, wrestle nude and be serviced orally...by both of us. We have a cabin in the woods...so call our box number and let's have a good time," Kenneth proudly concluded.

Marsha stood up, crossed the room and picked up Kenneth's writing. "Serviced orally by BOTH of us?" she questioned.

"That's just a come on Mother, honest," Kenneth replied.

"Really? What about seeking a black male?"

"Uh...that's my true fantasy Mother," Kenneth admitted. "The truth is no warrior in this country has faced more battles or been tested as much," he explained. "A black man at least ten years my senior produces the most potent of all essence. Hell, just to survive he must be tough, crafty, strong and persevering. His essence is without dispute the best! You said ask for the best Mother...and I love chocolate...what could be more delicious than a nice big chocolate cock?"

Marsha suppressed her urge to laugh and studied Kenneth for several moments before giving back his ad.

"Is it okay? Can I submit it Mother?" he pleaded.

"If you promise to get very hard and try your best to please Mother tonight, then yes Kenneth you may submit it," Marsha responded.

Kenneth was truly more excited than he had been in weeks. He carefully completed and submitted his ad then enthusiastically attacked Marsha. Licking her to climax then finishing up with his usual missionary quickie.

Over the next four weeks Kenneth had only three serious responses to his ad. The first was a black man that weighed over three hundred and sixty pounds, who wanted to be worshipped. The next one was gay and the third was a young hustler. Kenneth absorbed the disappointment and kept his ad running but began checking his box only twice a week. Marsha put the whole business out of her mind and made the most out of her life by molding Kenneth into the perfect househusband and personal slave.

Chapter five

*A*cross town, Raymond Jenkins sat in a buffet restaurant and watched his current girlfriend pig out. In between bites, she put down the food, the restaurant, Ray, all her ex's and life in general. She bragged about "going off" on different people then bitched about the baggage attached to her life. Ray tuned her out and wondered why he had such incredibly bad luck with women. He had just turned 40 and was divorced, with one grown daughter who stopped speaking to him when she dropped out of college and he stopped supporting her. Raymond Jenkins was a well paid, but unappreciated maintenance foreman with a large manufacturing company. He lived in a comfortable apartment, had money in the bank and owned a late model car. For the most part Ray was easy going and happy but only seemed to attract women weighing over two hundred and fifty pounds, or women with sizable attitudes and tons of baggage. As far as Ray was concerned this woman he was having dinner with was tolerated only because she was one step better than a street whore. An easy lay but that's all she was. Ray longed for a meaningful relationship, something special and shared. All the women he seemed to meet immediately see him as a wallet and/or captive audience for their tales of woe. And all of them soon stick out either their hand or finger. Asking for everything while bringing nothing but misery and chaos with them.

Ray was in no mood for company. After dinner he dropped his still chattering girlfriend off at her place then headed for home. At a stoplight he noticed an adult bookstore, so he turned into the parking lot and went into the store. After browsing for several minutes he bought one magazine then went home. For close to an hour that evening Ray smoked marijuana and channel surfed before getting bored and clicked off the television. He picked up his newly purchased magazine, The Tri-State Swingers Directory, admired the woman on the cover then skimmed through it. He looked at a few photo ads, chuckled at some and briefly pondered others before tossing the magazine aside and going to bed.

It was nearly two weeks later before Raymond Jenkins again picked up The Tri-State Swingers Directory. High on marijuana, drunk on brandy, lonely, horny and frustrated with his sex life, Ray was fantasizing about non-conventional relationships. Perhaps wonderful sex freaks who only wanted to service him. Or maybe something special...something to really enjoy. He carefully read each photo ad first then the smaller ads without photos. It was there that he came across Kenneth's ad. "Thirty something white couple seeking forty something black male. Veteran...well that's me so far," Ray commented.

"Straight...yeah cool. Divorced...uh huh. Must like to fish...oh yeah I'm with that! Hum...wrestle nude...hum...that's kinda freaky, but shit...why not! Hum...be serviced orally by both of us...oh hell yeah! That's what I'm talking about! Sheeit! Hum...cabin in the fucking woods...oh yeah...shit I gotta think on this one! I mean, hey I'm there...no gotta think on it first...shit!" Ray circled Kenneth's ad, dog-eared the page then put the magazine aside. He raided the refrigerator, stumbled to bed and quickly went fast asleep.

Several days later Ray again picked up the magazine and went immediately to the marked page, he re-read Kenneth's ad then composed a response. "Hi my name's Ray. I'm 40, a black man and I like your ad. I am divorced, an Air Force vet, live alone, 5'11", 168, love to fish, wrestled in high school and still pretty damn good! I'm straight, have staying power, need and absolutely love to be serviced orally. Either is welcome but both of you going down on me at the same time is an extremely erotic thought. Good times begin when you reel in this sweet chocolate trouser trout by contacting me on my numeric pager. I'm in maintenance, have the pager with me at all times and will get right back to you. Pager number 999 487-7732. I'm waiting, RAY." After reading his response Ray grinned then broke out in laughter. He fixed a drink, sat back down, picked up the phone and delivered the message exactly as written into Kenneth's voice mailbox.

Following dinner, two days later Kenneth casually checked his swinger line voice mail. He was surprised and absolutely overjoyed with Ray's message. A black man, a veteran, knows how to wrestle, loves to fish, needs to be serviced, seven years his senior...a perfect match, or so he thought. After more than a day of begging, Kenneth all but came in his pants and literally danced a jig when Mother gave him permission to respond. He dialed with lighting speed and entered his phone number then paced nervously for several minutes until Ray answered the page. For some reason Kenneth was startled when the phone rang. He fumbled for it before answering. "Hello?"

"Hi this is Ray...someone just paged me from this number."

"Uh yes. Uh...you answered our ad in The Swingers Directory," Kenneth responded.

"Aw yeah...ha-ha...sho did!" Ray chuckled. "You for real huh?"

"Uh...yeah," Kenneth replied.

"Well shit...good! I need to be serviced a lot. You with that?" Ray questioned.

Kenneth was swept away. "Ye...yes sir...I need to be of service...sir," he gushed.

"Tell me about this cabin in the woods," Ray instructed.

"Uh...it's kinda out in the middle of nowhere, very secluded but close to a good fishing lake. It's a nice place to get away from everything and...and really enjoy," Kenneth offered hoping to make the cabin sound tantalizing.

"All right I'm with that, so you think you would enjoy sucking my dick? Knowing that I am not going to suck yours?" Ray asked.

"Oh yes sir! Yes sir! Yes I would..." Kenneth swooned. "But I must have permission from my wife and she wants to talk to you...okay sir?" he asked.

"Sure...great! Put her on," Ray replied.

Marsha took the phone and soon found herself engaged in a pleasant, friendly conversation that quickly turned cozy and teasingly erotic. To Kenneth's dismay she talked for close to an hour before agreeing to meet Ray at a popular restaurant and bar.

In spite of their long phone conversation Marsha was somewhat ill at ease with the meeting. Since none of them had ever laid eyes on the other, Ray agreed to dress in a black shirt, black pants and tan suede vest. With most of the customers in the restaurant being white he should have been easy to spot. Yet Marsha and Kenneth sat at a table and stretched their necks looking for several minutes before spotting Ray happily chatting at the bar. When Kenneth meekly approached, Ray quickly put him at ease then joined them at their table.

Kenneth was extremely horny for male flesh, even more so for his ultimate fantasy male flesh. At this moment Raymond Jenkins was that fantasy male and Kenneth could barely contain himself, openly ogling Ray. Marsha instantly liked Ray, his baritone voice and easygoing manner not only charmed and aroused her, it stirred something deep within and she wanted to get to know him better. But…Kenneth repeatedly interrupted their conversation begging for permission to explain Ancient Greco Wrestling. Finally Marsha placed her hand on Ray's, looked deep into his eyes then smiled and gave her husband permission. Kenneth eagerly explained the wrestling rules then stared at Ray who smiled, but said nothing.

"You understand the rules?" Kenneth asked.

"Sure!" Ray responded, still smiling.

"And you're willing to wrestle by those rules?" Kenneth questioned with great hope.

"Sure...why not?" Ray replied.

"You understand you must pay the consequences if you lose?" Kenneth warned.

"I ain't gonna lose!" Ray shot back...his smile now a grin.

"Kenneth's a pretty good wrestler," Marsha put in.

"He is huh? Well I don't care how good he is...the stakes are too high for me to lose," Ray replied, playing with Marsha's hand as he spoke.

"You want to wrestle tonight?" Kenneth eagerly inquired.

"Kenneth!" Marsha snapped, "It's already late in the evening and I'm sure Ray has to work tomorrow just as we do."

"Yup...sure do," Ray agreed.

"How bout tomorrow...it's Friday," Kenneth hopefully offered.

"Kenneth!" Marsha scolded.

"Well actually I gotta work Saturday but no big thing...I can hang for a few hours tomorrow if you really want to get something on," Ray replied.

Kenneth stared pleadingly at Marsha who frowned at him then smiled at Ray. Marsha really liked Ray and she liked the feel of her hand being lightly stroked by his. At the same time however for some unexplained reason she was slightly intimidated and felt somewhat overpowered by this man. She knew she would never be able to control him as she had Kenneth and David and she had wanted their first private meeting to be at the cabin. But, like her panting husband, Marsha did not want to wait. She wanted to be alone with Ray and soon. So with nervous anticipation she invited him to their home the following evening.

Friday evening Marsha was jittery and nervous. She silently scolded herself and for the first time in weeks sniffed cocaine then fretted over her looks and what she should wear. Meanwhile, Kenneth inspected his newly purchased wrestling mat and paced anxiously around the house until the doorbell rang. Ray scored major points by arriving with an imported cigar for Kenneth and flowers for Marsha. Thrilled with the beautiful flowers and his thoughtfulness Marsha briefly hugged Ray. She felt a warm shiver seize her the instant their bodies made contact. She liked the feeling but after only a moment backed away and permitted Kenneth to thank Ray for his gift. Kenneth did so by dropping to one knee with great flourish then kissing both of Ray's hands.

Quickly becoming friends they settled in the den. Kenneth served drinks while Ray and Marsha charmed each other with engaging conversation. They chatted easily, immediately comfortable while discussing a range of subjects. Kenneth was anxious and wanted to wrestle; while Marsha was completely infatuated and found herself wishing she and Ray were alone. Several minutes later she could take no more of Kenneth's pleading, staring and panting all while she resisted a powerful urge to pull this wonderful man into her arms. She sighed deeply, smiled at Ray then gave Kenneth permission to challenge him.

Kenneth leapt to his feet and unrolled his new wrestling mat. He stood in the center of it and spoke in a loud voice, "This mat is dedicated to the honor and glory of true manhood as demonstrated by the art of Ancient Greco Wrestling. The rules are simple. Step on the mat totally naked, completely oil your body, keep the action on the mat, then revel in victory or properly honor the man that defeats you. Now...If you think you are man enough Raymond...step on the mat!" he concluded.

"If I think I'm man enough?" Ray responded with indignation. "Naw...naw, you shouldn't have said that see! Now I'm not gonna show any mercy. Man enough...ain't that a bitch! I'll show you something about man enough!" Ray slipped out of his shoes, stood up and began removing his clothes.

Marsha hurried out to the kitchen for snacks and more ice. When she returned to the den both men were completely naked, standing at opposite ends of the mat covering themselves with mineral oil. She took one look at Ray and immediately felt faint. Marsha had just settled into a chair when Kenneth offered to oil Ray's backside in exchange for the same.

"Like hell!" Ray retorted.

"Well we got to be completely oiled...uh Mother uh...would you help us," Kenneth pleaded.

Marsha took a deep breath before quickly oiling Kenneth's backside then Ray's. She collapsed back into the chair and drew her legs up tight to her body. The sight of Ray's naked body was causing Marsha to flashback to her childhood and the summers at her grandparent's farm. Every year for the first seventeen years of her life, Marsha and her brother spent the entire summer on that farm. During her fourteenth year, she was playing in the bunkhouse and discovered a large knothole that could be removed, providing an excellent peephole. With the knot removed she had clear view of most of the room including the open shower stalls. The bunkhouse was used by the farmhands that worked only when needed. Occasionally they stayed a few days but no one actually lived there. Mostly the farmhands used the bunkhouse to shower and/or drink liquor and play cards after working.

A few days later Marsha was at the peephole when the farmhands retired for the day and filed into the bunkhouse. She watched with wide-eyed astonishment as each of them completely undressed then showered. All of them were black men in their thirties and forties with bodies well defined by hard work. Those five black farmhands were the first men Marsha had actually seen totally naked. She was in awe, completely fascinated and made it her business to be at the knothole every time they showered.

The following summer she picked right up where she left off, spying often and enjoying it more. About mid-summer she was at the knothole excited, fingering herself and watching the three men inside. Two of the men where in the shower but the third was still undressing. He undressed very slowly because on his way into the bunkhouse he saw Marsha peeping. Once inside he spotted her eye in the knothole so he waited until both of the other men dressed and left, before he took off the remainder of his clothes, stood naked and stretched. He made sure Marsha was still watching then slowly stroked himself nearly hard. Next he walked back and forth, close to the knothole then away, his cock flopping and bouncing in front of him. Marsha was frozen to the knothole as she watched the farmhand take a shower. First he lathered his body, then slowly lathered and stroked his cock before rinsing and drying his body. On fire with lusty passion Marsha fled before the man left the bunkhouse but returned nearly every time the farmhands did.

After several solo performances by the same man Marsha finally realized that he knew she was watching. Her first instinct was to run away right then but she didn't. So for the remainder of that summer and over the next two that same farmhand continued to perform for her. Occasionally teasing and enticing her by standing close to the knothole and stroking himself hard.

On an ordinary Saturday during her sixteenth year Marsha faked sick to avoid going into town for supplies with her grandpa, brother and cousin. Shortly after noon she got out of bed and dressed. Not finding her grandma in the house, Marsha wandered around the farm before winding up at the bunkhouse. She expected it to be empty but thought she heard noises and immediately went to the knothole. Marsha was in utter shock when she removed the knot and saw her grandmother locked in a passionate embrace with one of the farmhands. She watched in disbelief as they kissed while his strong black hands slid up and down her grandma's back, squeezing and massaging her ass. Marsha was breathing hard when grandma dropped to her knees and pulled the man's pants and shorts down exposing his large black cock. She was relieved that it was not the same farmhand that entertained her and felt a slight tinge of jealously when her grandma eagerly closed her lips around the farmhands cock and began sucking. She sucked him with obvious enthusiasm before they completely undressed and settled onto a bunk. Grandma pumped his big meaty black cock with both hands then vigorously sucked it again before the farmhand rolled over. He raised Grandma's legs and pushed his big hard-on into her while she cried out and raised her hips to meet him. With but a few strokes he pushed all the way in and they fucked with a smooth even rhythm. They were positioned perfectly for Marsha to see everything in detail and see she did. Witnessing actual fucking for the first time in her life. Her panties were wet when the couple finished with a wild crescendo, kissing and clutching at each other while that big black cock smoothly slid in and out. The raw passion that possessed both lovers as they rode their cresting wave of mutual climax then floated into afterglow mesmerized Marsha. She was transfixed as grandma and her farmhand cuddled and whispered for several minutes before slowly separating. Marsha replaced the knot and ran back to the house, never speaking a word to anyone about what she had seen in the bunkhouse, and never missing an opportunity to spy through the knothole.

The bunkhouse performances by Marsha's farmhand became longer and more intimate her final year on the farm. On two separate occasions the man stood close to the knothole and stroked his cock to completion, actually cumming but within a scant few inches of Marsha's watchful eye. Both times it drove her wild with raw gritty lust and made her fight hard against the demanding impulse she felt to rush into the bunkhouse and melt into strong arms. For three long summers Marsha wished over and over that her farmhand would push his big brown cock through the knothole so she could touch it…but he never did.

During the spring of her eighteenth year, Marsha was hurt and angry when her grandparents sold the farm and moved to the nearby town. Deeply disappointed she briefly mourned then accepted her loss. At eighteen, school, boys and becoming a young adult had consumed her life. Over time memories of the farm and naked farmhands slipped deep into her subconscious...until now! The sight of this naked black man instantly brought those memories back in a flood. Taken by surprise Marsha was extremely uncomfortable and searching for common ground. She liked Ray a lot but now was afraid of him. She wanted to have sex with him and she wanted to live out her fantasies from the farm yet she was nervous and intimidated. Marsha was a timid and curious young virgin during that period when she spied through the knothole and looking at Ray made her feel that way now. She curled into a tighter ball as the timer clicked off its last second and the bell signaled the start of the wrestling match.

The timer was used to give each wrestler a few minutes of mental preparation time and to signal the start of the match. Kenneth had set it for five minutes instead of the usual three because he really liked Ray's firm naked body and wanted longer to ogle and admire him. He posed on one knee and stared at Ray who stretched his muscles then casually paced around his corner.

Kenneth said a silent prayer just as the bell sounded then sprang into a crouch and began circling Ray who stood still and watched him. Kenneth lunged and Ray sidestepped which caused Kenneth to run off the mat. He quickly returned, crouched and started circling Ray again. He lunged again and again Ray sidestepped this time tripping Kenneth and grabbing his leg during his fall. Ray quickly twisted Kenneth's leg around his and leaned his weight against it. Kenneth struggled hard, putting his other foot against Ray's ass for leverage but Ray did not appreciate the feeling. He twisted harder pulling Kenneth's leg backwards while applying more of his body weight.

The pain proved to be too much and Kenneth cried out, "Oh fuck! Ouch...okay, okay...I give!"

"You give? Give my ass! Get that other shoulder on the mat," Ray demanded.

Kenneth sighed deeply, winced in pain then flattened both his shoulders against the mat. "ONE...TWO..." Ray counted.

Instinctively Kenneth jerked one shoulder off the mat, causing Ray to twist as hard as he could.

"OUCH! FUCK! OUCH! SHIT...OH PLEASE! PLEASE!" Kenneth wailed then again pressed both his shoulders to the mat.

"ONE...TWO...THREE! MATCH OVER!" Ray sang out. He released his grip, stepped clear of Kenneth and stood with his hands on his hips. Kenneth scrambled to his knees, wincing at the pain in his leg. He positioned himself directly in front of Ray and looked up at him. "You are the best sir...the best! I salute you and beg permission to honor you...please sir?" He pleaded while licking his lips which were inches from Ray's cock.

Ray grinned. "Get busy son!" he replied.

Kenneth was literally quivering with desire when he touched his lips to Ray semi-hard cock. He quickly sucked it into his mouth and swirled his tongue around it while glowing red with absolute delight.

Ray looked down at Kenneth and smiled while Marsha tightly hugged a pillow and quietly watched. After a few moments Ray smiled at Marsha. "You want to join him," he asked.

"Next time," she replied weakly. "This time he must pay proper respect to the superior manhood that conquered him."

"You heard the lady son pay proper respect!" Ray demanded with a big smile. "Yeah...uh huh...ah yeah...now you showing some respect. Umm...uh huh...real good." Ray enjoyed the spoils of victory, grinding his hips while pumping his hard cock in and out of Kenneth's hungry mouth. He rubbed Kenneth's head and briefly allowed him to lick his balls then guided his cock back inside Kenneth's mouth. Without any assistance whatsoever Kenneth came hard. His cum splattered onto the mat, yet he held fast to Ray's thighs and sucked hard as Ray's swollen black cock pumped in and out of his mouth.

Marsha admired Ray's staying power but had seen all she could stand and slipped out of the room unnoticed. She didn't return to the den until the men had showered and were dressing. Kenneth was overjoyed and still eyeing Ray's crotch while Ray was satisfied with the blowjob but disappointed that Marsha wasn't in on it. They had another drink and chatted for several minutes before Ray's schedule forced him to call it a night.

As the three of them approached the front door, Kenneth dropped to his knees, buried his face in Ray's crotch, breathed hard several times then stepped several feet away and waved good-bye. Marsha lightly hugged Ray intending it to be brief but he pulled her close and held her against him. She hesitated then hugged him tightly for several long moments. Marsha's head was spinning. She felt tense, intimidated and greatly aroused. She never wanted to see Ray again yet she did not want him to leave. She pressed tighter against his body and dug her nails into his back. She was afraid to let him go because she knew he would come back and she would truly have to face the secrets of her youth. That thought scared and excited her more than any previous experience in her life and she was frozen in Ray's arms.

"You're driving me mad with desire for you gorgeous lady. Mad with desire to caress your soft naked flesh, mad to love and make endless love to you. I'm mad for beautiful Marsha and loving it," Ray whispered. He kissed her on the forehead, waved at Kenneth then slipped out the door.

At no time in her entire life had Marsha experienced any emotions this powerful. Shivers tore through her body, her heart fluttered; she felt faint and couldn't stop flashing back to the bunkhouse and her knothole. She ordered Kenneth to tidy up the house then went straight to bed but not to sleep. She lay wide awake for hours thinking only of the man on the other side of the knothole. That black, strong and very naked farmhand that eagerly displayed his delicious body then aroused and excited her with his performances. She fingered herself remembering how much she had truly loved him and how badly she had wanted him. She still wanted him and she knew he wanted her. Desperately she longed to be in his arms. She wanted to touch and taste his lips, feel his caresses, kiss his body, suck his smooth brown cock into her mouth then completely surrender to his superior strength and power as he enters her. Lightly perspiring and breathing hard she climaxed with a tremendous rush, tightly wrapped in the precious memory of her farmhand...only his face was now that of Raymond Jenkins.

Chapter six

Saturday morning Marsha awoke tense, very horny and ill at ease with her flash backs from the night before. She sat upright and watched Kenneth who was happily dressing.

He beamed at her. "Good morning Mother. You want coffee or breakfast?" he asked. Kenneth was jubilant and bubbling. "I've got an early tee time and it's a gorgeous day…"

"No I'll get something later…just go," Marsha responded. "And don't shoot lower than your boss. And Kenny…take your jacket."

Kenneth smiled, got his jacket, kissed Mother good-bye and headed to the golf course.

Marsha was relieved when he left because she wanted to be alone with her thoughts. Thoughts that soon turned to the naked black man that had wrestled her husband in their den the night before. Raymond Jenkins now held Marsha in complete fascination. She knew she could not resist his touch. In fact, she badly needed it but feared the effects he would have on her. He made her feel like a hot shy teenager. The same hot shy teenager that spied through the knothole and like her grandmother fell in love with a black man's body. Her thoughts and fingers produced a shuddering climax causing Marsha to cry out...more from relief than pleasure. Afterwards, she lay motionless considering many different scenarios then decided to avoid seeing Raymond Jenkins for as long as possible.

Marsha intentionally maxed out their social schedules and kept Ray on hold for close to three weeks before giving in to Kenneth's constant pleadings. She allowed Kenneth to page Ray but it was she who answered when the phone rang then chatted for close to forty minutes. The mutual attraction shared by Marsha and Ray was powerful, undeniable and very seductive. Blushing, she invited him to dinner the following Saturday then bid farewell.

Afterwards she carefully planned the entire evening. There would be no wrestling, Kenneth would dress in his towel wrap, a bow tie and shirt cuffs then serve as the houseboy throughout Ray's visit. Only if he did a good job, would Marsha consider allowing him to service Ray. Kenneth eagerly accepted her conditions; he badly wanted Ray's cock back in his mouth and would have agreed to most anything to get it.

Ray arrived early Saturday evening with a bottle of cognac. He was first greeted by Kenneth dressed in his houseboy uniform. He immediately dropped to his knees and buried his face into Ray's crotch, breathed deeply several times, then quickly stepped away. High on cocaine and dressed provocatively, Marsha gushed over Ray's compliments. She briefly hugged him then took his hand and led him to a backgammon table in the den. They enthusiastically chatted over a game of backgammon while Kenneth scurried about serving drinks and preparing dinner.

"What's with him? And that outfit?" Ray inquired.

"He is our houseboy tonight," Marsha replied.

"Is zat right?" Ray chuckled.

"Yes but he came with a price..." Marsha advised, "and I apologize for closing the deal without first consulting you?"

"What's the bottom line?" Ray questioned.

"I promised he could service you if he does a good job," Marsha replied.

"You did huh?" Ray inquired with a twinkle in his eye.

"I'm sorry..." Marsha apologized, "but it's not like I can't join in or limit his involvement."

"So he's working for a taste huh?"

"Yes I'm afraid he is," Marsha sighed.

"Then I have a suggestion."

"Which is?"

"Let's dine in the nude," Ray suggested.

"Perfect!" Marsha beamed. "I mean is that a great idea or what? I would love to dine naked."

When Kenneth announced dinner he was surprised but not excited when Mother stood up and done a slow sexy strip tease ending up completely nude. The show was for Ray so Kenneth watched with little interest until Mother ordered him to help Mr. Jenkins undress. It was music to Kenneth ears and he quickly helped Ray out of his clothes. Excited by their now naked dinner guest, Kenneth completely got into his roll. He lit candles, adjusted the lights and music then served the appetizers followed by salads. He quickly ate his meal in the kitchen then returned to the dining room in time to refill the wine and water glasses, remove the salad plates and serve the main course. Having completed his chores Kenneth quietly stood by waiting to serve dessert.

Both Marsha and Ray found it very heady and incredibly sexy to dine in the nude. They admired each other across a beautifully set table complete with fresh cut flowers. Soft music filled the air...the food was excellent, the wine superb and their private waiter performed flawlessly. Marsha couldn't stop blushing; she had never enjoyed any meal as much. Tripping on cocaine, she first imagined Ray to be the farmhand she had watched and wanted. Then she imagined herself a southern belle and the captive bride of a former slave that overthrew his master and conquered the plantation. The fact that Kenneth was at this moment their white slave-boy only helped this fantasy take root. Totally infatuated and intensely aroused, Marsha invited Ray to share their hot tub after dinner.

Despite his excellent performance as houseboy, Kenneth was resentful of seeing his wife entertain another man. His own raging desires overwhelmed his anxieties however and he carefully eyed Ray's cock throughout the evening. As soon as Marsha and Ray settled into the tub, Kenneth served cognac then as before quietly stood by.

Ray had been pleasantly surprised when Marsha quickly accepted his suggestion that they dine in the nude then followed through with it. He eased into the tub admiring her body and wishing time would just simply stop and leave him right there with her. Marsha sat facing Ray, sipped her drink and sniffed cocaine while Ray smoked a joint and Kenneth happily accepted little hits of both. For several minutes Marsha and Ray chatted and stared with lustful passion at the other. Then Marsha turned her body around, pressed her back to Ray's chest and settled into his arms. She completely lost herself to the peace flooding her soul as she continued to imagine belonging only to this wonderful man. For more than twenty minutes the pulsating water, the drugs and the comfort Marsha and Ray found within their closeness and the touch of their naked bodies, fueled and intensified their raging desire. Marsha was approaching an orgasm when she abruptly stepped from the tub, took Ray's hand and led him to the den.

Wrapped together in a large beach towel, Marsha and Ray snuggled on the sofa while Kenneth sat on the floor in front of them and stared at Ray's cock.

Marsha stroked Kenneth's head. "Has he been good? Does he deserve a taste?" she asked Ray.

"Yeah…I'd say he's been a pretty good houseboy tonight," Ray replied.

Kenneth flushed red, literally starving for the taste of cock. His own cock had been hard and dribbling cum onto his towel wrap since Ray undressed and he simply couldn't wait to get that big chocolate meat inside his mouth.

Marsha opened the towel and focused on Ray's cock and the beautiful black cock she had yearned for during her youth. She took it in her hand and lightly stroked it, thrilled that it grew larger and harder in her grip. Slowly her gazed shifted up Ray's body to his chest, then to his lips and finally deep into his eyes. Marsha was literally on fire inside when she released her hand from Ray's cock, gave Kenneth permission then touched her lips to Ray's.

They kissed lightly at first, savoring the moment and the taste of each other. But soon their kisses grew wet, hot and extremely passionate, sending shivers and jolts of delighted excitement through both of them. Their kiss was absolutely delicious and neither could get enough as they sank deeper into each other.

Kenneth meanwhile was gorging himself on Ray's cock, licking his balls, the shaft and the head, then swallowing as much as he could and sucking mightily.

Ray was hard and throbbing but nearly oblivious to Kenneth, he was completely captivated by Marsha as she was by him. Each was overwhelmed by the other as red-hot pent-up passion fueled their mutual lust.

Marsha was again approaching climax when Ray abruptly broke the kiss. "What the hell?" he exclaimed. Kenneth had came onto his towel wrap, Ray's leg and the carpet.

"KENNETH!" Marsha snapped.

"I'm sorry Mother! I'm sorry."

"Goddamn you Kenneth! Clean that up!" Marsha ordered. "NO! DON'T YOU DARE LICK IT! WASH IT OFF RAY AND SCRUB IT OFF THE CARPET...RIGHT NOW! THEN GO TO BED!"

Kenneth followed orders, quickly washing away his semen then going to bed. He regretted not having swallowed Ray's essence but was certain continued obedience would get him all he wanted. He had thoroughly enjoyed Ray's big cock and without any thought or concern about leaving his wife naked and alone with another man, who was also naked, Kenneth settled into bed and quickly fell asleep with a contented smile on his face.

After Kenneth left the room Marsha felt a brief wave of panic...her plan had called for Kenneth to suck Ray off while she enjoyed his caresses. But Kenneth had let her down and she punished him without thinking. Now Ray had not gotten off and neither had she. Helplessly overwhelmed, she shared a glass of cognac with Ray then melted back into his arms. Ray was captivated by Marsha. She was soft, delicate and sweeter than any woman he had known. He couldn't get enough of her and she couldn't get enough of him. They sprawled comfortably on the sofa giggling, caressing and kissing. Ray briefly kissed Marsha's neck and breast, she loved it but needed his lips against hers and each time grabbed his head and guided his mouth back to her lips. Ray was lying on top of her when she raised and spread her legs. She chewed at his tongue and moaned, pleading for Ray to take her. He raised his ass, grabbed his cock and lightly tapped it against her clit. Marsha began to grind her hips and soon was again approaching climax as Ray tapped harder and faster. She broke the kiss and tightly gripped Ray's head as the first volley of orgasmic explosion ripped through her body. At precisely that moment Ray pushed his hard black cock into Marsha's wet quivering pussy. She arched her body and pushed upward to him, shuddering with orgasm and wanting more, desperately wanting him to take her...all of her. Ray raised her legs even more and then slowly, smoothly worked his hard-on inside her. She cried out and he hugged her to him, touched more deeply than ever by any woman.

Once again Marsha was a hot shy teenager only this time she was not spying through the knothole. This time she was inside the bunkhouse, in bed with her black lover and he was taking her virginity. Marsha was incredulous with the physical size of Ray's cock. This was a man, more than twice as big as Kenneth and certainly the most she had ever taken. His cock explored new territory within her, penetrating deeper than she had ever been touched while fulfilling her completely. She sucked Ray's lips, stroked his back and floated in pure ecstasy as he pumped deeper into her, providing the most glorious sexual feelings she had ever experienced. Ray took his time and savored each minute. Frequently stopping to passionately kiss Marsha and stare into her eyes.

It was the ultimate shared bliss for both of them but Marsha could barely contain herself because of the certain knowledge that...that missing something was no longer missing. She wiped the perspiration from Ray's face with her hands and pumped her hips in time with his increasingly powerful thrust, lost solely to the moment. Several happy minutes later Ray exploded inside her with such intensity Marsha soared on his momentum and climaxed yet again.

They did not disconnect, they couldn't instead they lay in the others embrace, kissing, nuzzling, talking and falling in love. After a short while Ray again grew hard inside of Marsha. She was thrilled and they changed positions so Marsha could sit astride Ray and slowly make love. She wanted to look at him, run her fingers across his dark brown chest and watch his big, hard black cock slid in and out of her quivering white flesh. Marsha was completely swept away and in total awe. She had never experienced anything near what she now felt and she loved Ray for his staying power which gave her plenty of time to enjoy it. For several minutes she slowly slid up and down then following a long deep grind they changed positions onto their sides and fucked with a smooth funky rhythm. Happy and excited, Marsha hungrily kissed Ray while he stroked her back, pumped into her and returned her wet kisses.

Ray was enjoying the best sexual experience of his life. Having already cum once, he felt confident in his ability to control the second climax until Marsha began breathing really hard and cried out, "Oh Ray...Ray! Take me master! TAKE ME! Oh...oh, oh...RAAY!"

It was too much, Ray held Marsha tight and she held tight to him, both exploding again and again, suspended in intense climax. They melted into each other and soared in afterglow for nearly thirty minutes before Ray decided to leave. Ray had to leave because he suddenly realized that he might drift off to sleep. If he went to sleep with this wonderful woman in his arms and she was still there when he awoke, he wasn't giving her back. In spite of how badly he wanted to keep her, Marsha was a married woman...and they were both spent...very happy and very spent. It had been the greatest evening ever and it was time to say goodnight.

Standing at the front door with Marsha in his arms Ray fought the strong urge to pick her up and carry her home with him, while Marsha fought her own strong urge to bar the door and never let him leave. For close to twenty minutes they hugged, kissed and said good-bye before Ray felt himself getting hard yet again. He held Marsha tight, kissed her deeply with all the true love he felt for her then vanished out the door, leaving her breathless and stunned.

The following day Marsha suffered. Her body loudly cried out for more of Raymond Jenkins and that fact was difficult for her to deal with. She had not intended to sleep with him but the evening had gotten out of hand. Now she was on a major guilt trip and involuntarily flashing back on her grandmother making love to a black man in the bunkhouse. She stayed in bed until early afternoon ordering Kenneth about and trying to come to grips with the experiences of the previous night. She tried mightily to deny her feelings for Ray and by late evening Kenneth had become the scapegoat and held completely responsible. Marsha berated Kenneth but had no energy to punish him. She was lost in the mysteries of human relationships, having been touched deeper and more meaningfully than ever before.

Over the next two days Marsha attempted to rationalize her behavior and desires, before finally deciding that Kenneth, cocaine, cognac and Raymond Jenkins were responsible for her being in this position. Kenneth had let her down, not done his job and caused embarrassment. Cocaine and cognac had taken possession of her common sense and Ray Jenkins blurred her focus in a tangle of complex emotions. She would punish Kenneth, moderate her consumption of cognac and completely eliminate both cocaine and Raymond Jenkins from her life. Her being and body yearned for this man more than anyone she had ever known, but she was afraid to let herself be herself.

Marsha was honestly intimidated by her need and feelings for Raymond Jenkins. She knew she could not resist or share this man with her husband. She wanted him all to herself or not at all, so she decided that Ray could become Kenneth's new fishing buddy. A fishing buddy invited to the cabin only, on fishing trips that absolutely would not include her. Marsha swallowed a valium and prayed that Ray would accept his new role of occasional fishing buddy and that Kenneth would come home charged up and horny like he did after a fishing trip with David. She ended the prayer asking for relief from her intimidation of and intense desire for Raymond Jenkins. Marsha was now seeking to return her marriage and sex life to its safe nearly non-existing state.

When Kenneth mustered the courage to ask if Ray was being included in their weekend plans, Marsha punished him for his behavior during Ray's previous visit. Denial, hurt, anger and defeat were among the many frustrations Marsha unsuccessfully tried to release by giving Kenneth several hard lashes across his bare ass with her wide leather belt. Kenneth endured his punishment then jumped for joy when Mother announced that Ray had been approved as a suitable play-buddy and could be invited on a fishing trip. She made it clear that Ray was now Kenneth's fishing buddy and no longer welcome at their house. She would not be going on any fishing trips with them and wasn't interested in hearing about the trips either. This bit of news only made Kenneth happier; he immediately phoned and invited Ray on a fishing trip the coming weekend, happily lying when Ray asked if Marsha was going.

Eager to get out of the city and especially eager to get Marsha back into his arms, Ray accepted Kenneth's invitation then cleared his schedule. Going on a fishing trip was a wonderful break and Ray was really looking forward to a weekend in the woods. Shortly after noon on Friday he happily packed a small bag then impatiently waited. Ray had not been fishing in some time and was anxious to get a line in the water but was disappointed to find Kenneth alone in the Jeep. "Where's Marsha?" he asked.

"She's working on an important assignment which she has to finish because it's due for litigation on Monday, shouldn't take her but a few hours. She didn't want to delay our weekend so she told me to pick you up and go ahead. She will drive up later tonight," Kenneth lied.

"Bummer!" Ray sighed then adjusted his seat, relaxed and settled in for the long ride.

They arrived early in the evening, opened the cabin, collected their fishing gear and set off to catch dinner. They had chatted about a range of subjects on the drive up and Ray had become a little more at ease with Kenneth. He couldn't understand Kenneth's desire for a man when he had a magnificent woman in Marsha but kept his thoughts to himself. Just before darkness approached they returned to the cabin with the best of their catch. Kenneth made drinks, cleaned the fish and prepared dinner, while Ray made a fire then relaxed. As soon as dinner was over, Kenneth challenged Ray to the wrestling mat, but Ray declined saying, "Shouldn't you call Marsha? See what's up with her?"

"There's no phone here...and no reason to worry...she'll let us know if something is wrong," Kenneth responded.

"How's she gonna do that if there's no phone here?" Ray demanded.

"Because you have your pager...don't you?"

"Hum...as a matter of fact I do," Ray chuckled.

"She knew you would and said she would page us if she has a problem," Kenneth lied. "She probably finished late and is going to drive up in the morning. I really doubt she will drive up tonight yet."

Ray wasn't happy; he looked at his pager, declined another invitation to wrestle but agreed to play chess. It took nearly two hours for the match to end in hopeless stalemate.

Kenneth was annoyed and anxious. Ray had blocked his every move and he hated stalemates. "THERE'S ONLY ONE WAY TO SETTLE THIS BATTLE! UNLESS YOUR BLACK ASS IS CHICKENSHIT! I'LL SEE YOU ON THE MAT!" he bellowed.

Ray chuckled, "All right...silly motherfucker! Bring yo ass on!"

Kenneth quickly unrolled the mat, undressed and began oiling his body.

Ray slowly undressed and reluctantly began applying oil. "What's with this oil shit anyway?" he complained.

"It's the original rules," Kenneth explained. "It makes it harder to grip your opponent. Here I'll oil your back then you can oil mine."

"Like hell you will!" Ray snorted.

"Come on Ray...we gotta be completely oiled!" Kenneth whined.

"You can forget about feeling up my ass. Just pour the shit in the middle of your back and let it run down, this ain't gonna take long anyway," Ray instructed.

Kenneth reluctantly accepted Ray's oiling method then set the timer. Again he set it for five minutes and again he dropped to one knee and ogled Ray. When the bell sounded, Kenneth said his silent prayer, jumped into his crouch and began circling. Ray stood still and carefully watched until Kenneth lunged, then ducked under him, grabbed both his legs and rose up, dumping Kenneth flat on his back. Ray smothered him with his body weight, forced Kenneth's shoulders to the mat and counted.

"ONE...TWO...THREE! Just like that!" He stepped free of Kenneth. "You happy now bitch?" he asked.

Kenneth scrambled to his knees, "I'm honored sir...you are the best, the absolute best! I'm honored to be on the same mat with you. May I show respect sir...please?"

Ray grinned, "I want you to suck it nice and slow son, get it real hard so I can slide it down your throat and fuck your face," he instructed.

Kenneth followed orders with ripples of delight flooding his body while his mouth sucked in Ray's big chocolate cock. He sucked enthusiastically for several minutes before getting it really hard. When he did, Ray grabbed Kenneth's head and forced his hard-on deep into his throat until Kenneth's nose was pressed tight against his crotch. Kenneth had never deep throated a cock, he didn't know he could. Goose bumps seized him as his mouth and throat muscles automatically responded, sucking and massaging this delicious invader. He flushed red, dug his fingers into Ray's hips and came hard while trying to suck him in even deeper. Ray was impressed and grinned. His cock grew even bigger and his cum began to build while he thrilled to the hot wet mouth and deep slick throat servicing him. Actually, Ray intended to punish Kenneth by forcing his cock into his throat, but Kenneth liked it, adjusted and performed extremely well. He was overjoyed when cum exploded from Ray and savored every drop that slid down his throat.

"Oh Yeah!" Ray sang out. "Now that's what I call a real face fucking! How bout you? You like that son?" he asked.

"Um hum," Kenneth hummed around the big cock still filling his mouth.

A few minutes later, Ray stepped into the shower then stepped right out, bitching and cursing about the cold water.

"That's all we have here," Kenneth offered.

"Why the fuck don't you get a hot water heater?" Ray snapped. "Cheap motherfucker! Shit!"

Kenneth soothed Ray by heating water which Ray used to take a sponge bath. Afterwards he stretched, drank a nightcap then climbed into bed.

"Ray…can I sleep with you?" Kenneth asked.

"Hell naw! Don't even think about!" Ray replied. He relaxed but stayed awake and watched Kenneth until he settled into the single bed and went to sleep.

The following morning Ray awoke to the smell of bacon frying. Kenneth served breakfast, cleaned up afterwards then pleaded with Ray to go fishing. But Ray was concerned about Marsha so Kenneth drove eight miles to a general store, went straight to the pay phone and called his office. He pretended to talk to Marsha then got back in the Jeep and told Ray she was still working on this important assignment. "She's a legal researcher," Kenneth explained. "A trial starts next week and she must have the research done by Monday. She hopes to wrap it up shortly after noon and hit the road.

She also said if she doesn't arrive or page before night fall, she wasn't coming and to have a good time."

Ray wasn't surprised. By now he figured Marsha wasn't coming and decided to just enjoy being away in the woods. They bought some fresh bait, returned to the cabin, collected their gear, hiked to the lake and spent the day fishing. By late afternoon Kenneth had cleaned and cooked several fish but they continued to catch more.

Their bellies were full, they were high on marijuana, drinking beer and joking when Kenneth got serious. "Ray? I'm really sorry Marsha hasn't got here yet," he lied.

"Yeah...I bet you are!" Ray responded.

"Can I ask you something?"

"What?"

"Have you ever done a guy?"

"Done a guy?" Ray chuckled. "What does that mean?"

"You know...have you ever drilled a guy?" Kenneth explained.

"You mean have I ever fucked a dude?"

"Yeah! Have you?" Kenneth asked hopefully.

"Yeah as a matter of fact I did a few years back...why?"

"Tell me about it...please?" Kenneth pleaded.

"Tell you about it? Ain't shit to tell...happened a long time ago," Ray snapped.

"Please Ray...please...I beg you...tell me about it! Please!"

Ray chuckled, leaned back against a rock and rolled a joint.

"I'll do anything," Kenneth promised. "Anything at all if you tell me about it."

Ray reeled in a small fish, looked it over then threw it back. "Kenneth? You a pain in the ass, you know that?" he grumbled.

"I'm sorry Ray...please tell me...please?" Kenneth begged in earnest.

"All right, all right...goddamn!" Ray snapped. "It happened back when I was in the Air Force. I was stationed in North Dakota, Minot Air Force Base. Colder than twelve motherfuckers up there and no women. There was a couple of little towns pretty close to the base, but there wasn't nothing but fat Indian broads in them and those stupid horny GI's had spoiled them fat broads rotten. You had to beg and pay. I was stuck there for eighteen months and didn't have no car so I decided to fuck my hand and save my money. After I had been there about six months I came in after duty one day and discovered I had a new roommate. I had been lucky and had the whole room to myself, and I didn't really want a roommate but there wasn't shit I could do about it. Anyway, my new roomy was a little white dude from the east coast named Joey Branch. He was nervous and scared of everything so I tried to make him feel welcome and gave up his share of the room."

"In them days the barracks were dormitories with long hallways, two or three men to a room, a dayroom in the middle and a large latrine on each end. We usually undressed in our rooms and went to the shower wearing nothing but a towel. A couple days after Joey moved in I was getting ready to take a shower and I noticed him staring at my dick when I undressed. I blew it off at first but kept noticing him staring every time I undressed. Finally one night, I was loaded and horny, I undressed and Joey stared. I showered and returned to the room, took off my towel and walked around naked. Joey's eyes followed my every move so I said, "you see something you like Joey?" He blushed and looked away, then in a little tiny voice said yes. So I asked if he liked what he was looking at well enough to taste it. He said yes again and slid off the bunk onto his knees, so I stepped in front of him and pushed my dick into his mouth. It was the first time a man had sucked my dick and Joey's mouth felt terrific. Course I hadn't had any pussy in months. It didn't take long before I came in his mouth and he swallowed all of it and liked it. So after that whenever I wanted a blowjob all I had to do was show Joey my dick. Sometimes that little punk would wake me up early and suck my dick before work," Ray chuckled as he lit the joint. He took several drags then passed it to Kenneth.

"One night I had guard duty and got in late," Ray continued, "it was raining really hard, thundering and shit. Joey was scared as hell. He was afraid of thunder and asked if he could sleep in my bed with me. I laughed and told him that wasn't a good idea cause I fuck anybody that sleeps with me. I climbed into bed and just as I almost got to sleep another big thunderclap woke me up. A few minutes later I felt Joey ease into my bed. I turned over and he backed his naked ass right up against my dick, so I felt for his asshole then pushed my dick into it. He was tight and greasy, must have lubed his ass with something. I pushed and kept pushing until my dick slid deep inside him. It was freaky and felt good so I rolled on top and fucked him while he lay on his stomach and pumped his ass to me. He moaned real softly the whole time I fucked him. He liked it. Liked it too much in fact, ole Joey was my bitch for real after that and he wanted me to fuck him a lot...but I didn't. I let him suck my dick pretty regular but I only fucked him three more times during the rest of my tour. Joey was okay, a lot better than my hand or those fat Indian broads but I was happy as hell to get outta there," Ray concluded.

"Didn't you hate to leave Joey?" Kenneth asked.

"Hell naw!" Ray declared. "I was glad to get away from his ass and get some real pussy. My last week he acted liked a little bitch. He cried and wanted me to fuck him every night...really pissed me off so I introduced him to a buddy of mine. Big ole mule dick brother named Stanley Johnson. The Indian broads use to run from Stanley cause his dick was so big...ha-ha. He swore it was at least twelve inches long but I can't say for sure. I got enough of my own so I wasn't really interested. Anyway, I invited Stanley to our room and arranged it so that he walked in while Joey was sucking my dick. Joey was scared and embarrassed until I made him suck Stanley. I could tell he really liked Stanley's big meat so I told Stanley to fuck him while he sucked me. When Stanley's dick pushed into his ass Joey really freaked, he wailed and moaned then quickly sucked me dry. After that he did some serious fucking, humping and grinding his ass until he got every bit of Stanley's big monster dick up his butt. Stanley was just as thrilled. They hit it right off and Joey moved into Stanley's room the next day. Just before I left Stanley told me he would rather fuck Joey than any bitch he knew, because he rarely got to put even half of his big meat into most women while Joey took every inch and loved it. Then he gave me fifty bucks as thanks," Ray chuckled, "and fifty bucks was a lot of money back then."

"Where did you go when you left North Dakota?" Kenneth asked.

"Home on leave, then to the Philippines."

"Did you ever hear from Joey?" Kenneth questioned.

"Yeah a couple of times," Ray replied. He wrote to thank me for being a great roommate and for turning him on to Stanley. Apparently they had it going on pretty good cause they both volunteered for Thule."

"What's Thule?" Kenneth asked.

"Thule Greenland, coldest motherfucker on earth," Ray responded. "Everything is in one high rise building up there cause yo ass will sho nuff freeze up if you're outside for long. The Air Force offered extra money and rank for a tour of eighteen months and Stanley and Joey went up there together. I never heard from them again, so I don't know what became of them, but I'll bet Joey's ass never froze up though," he chuckled.

Kenneth's eyes were shining, "Did you ever suck Joey?" he asked.

"Hell naw!" Ray snapped.

"You've never sucked a guy have you Ray?"

"Hell naw and I ain't going to!" Ray responded.

"It's a great experience, the best...really!" Kenneth gushed.

"Yeah...well I'll take your word for that son," Ray replied.

"It's so good...anytime you want me to, I'll suck you Ray!" Kenneth offered.

"No shit," Ray snorted.

"I'm serious...I'd really like to suck you right now! No wrestling or anything...just whip it out and let me suck it okay?" Kenneth beamed.

"Maybe later. Think there's any chance Marsha's waiting for us at the cabin?" Ray asked.

"It's possible...you ready to head back?" Kenneth sighed.

"Yeah...in a few minutes...got more fish than we can eat anyway," Ray responded.

Ray was disappointed when they arrived back at the cabin and Marsha was not there. He sat on the porch, picked up a large piece of wood and began whittling.

"You're pretty good at that?" Kenneth declared.

"Use to whittle a lot when I was a kid...my grandfather taught me how," Ray explained.

"It's warm enough and there's nobody around for miles so we can get naked and be comfortable if we want to," Kenneth advised.

"I'm okay for now," Ray assured.

"Goddamn you Ray! I'm dying here..." Kenneth snapped. "If you won't let me suck you...you can at least let me see it!"

"Kenneth! You something else man! Oh what the fuck!" Ray grumbled then took off his clothes. "Fold these up!" he ordered, handing Kenneth his clothes. "Now stare all the fuck you want."

"Thank you sir...gawd...you're so fucking gorgeous," Kenneth gushed.

"Back the fuck off! I said you could stare, not slobber on!" Ray barked.

Kenneth put the clothes away, undressed then pranced about but Ray ignored him and continued to sit on the porch and whittle.

As sunset approached, Kenneth sat down on the porch step below Ray. "It's going to be a great sunset," he said.

"It is at that," Ray agreed, putting aside his carving.

"That's really good work, I mean it," Kenneth praised, while inspecting the carving.

"Why thank you but it's nowhere near finished," Ray replied.

"Ray I'd be the happiest man in America if you opened your legs and let me cradle my head on your lap as we watch this beautiful sunset. I won't try anything, I promise. It's just that everything is so beautiful. This trip, you, the fishing, your carving, the sunset...I just want to cuddle up and absorb it all," Kenneth pleaded.

Ray opened his legs and allowed Kenneth to nestle his head. They were motionless for a few moments then Ray stroked Kenneth head inspiring him to nuzzle Ray's cock as they watched the setting sun in silence.

Just as the sun slipped below horizon, Kenneth kissed Ray's cock several times then asked, "Ray? Will you drill me?"

"What? Drill you?"

"Yeah... you know."

"Oh, now you want me to fuck you huh?" Ray quizzed.

"Will you? Please?" Kenneth begged.

"Hell naw!"

"Why not? Come on Ray...please?" Kenneth pleaded.

"Hell naw...that's a shitty deal at best!"

"I've got condoms," Kenneth offered.

"Uh huh…yo ass came well prepared didn't you?" Ray sourly observed.

"Please Ray…" Kenneth begged again. "You have no idea how bad I need to do this."

"Well if you need dick up your butt all that much why you bothering me instead of your fag brothers?" Ray demanded.

"It's not like that Ray, I've never had it up the ass," Kenneth admitted.

"Then why you need it up there now?"

"I've gotta have it Ray!" Kenneth insisted.

"Why?" Ray demanded.

"Cause…cause I have a close friend that has wanted me for a long time, a very long time and I want to be able to finally please him," Kenneth confessed.

"So why don't you get him to fuck you?"

"He tried, but I couldn't take it."

"Then what the fuck makes you think you can take me?" Ray questioned with indignant surprise.

"He backed off when he knew it was hurting me," Kenneth replied. "He doesn't want it if it hurts me…he lost his hard-on and everything."

"And you hoping I won't back off?" Ray concluded.

"I know if I can just get by that first little bit of pain I'm really going to like it. And yes, I am hoping you won't back off. Will you do it please? Please?" Kenneth pleaded again.

"Stop begging bitch!" Ray snapped then walked into the cabin and stretched out on the sofa. "The only way a man can bust a cherry asshole is because he really wants to. If I decide I want to I will…otherwise don't ask!" he instructed.

The certain knowledge that Kenneth wanted to get fucked instead of wanting to fuck him allowed Ray to really relax for the first time. He ordered Kenneth to build a fire and then give him a full body massage. Ray rolled a joint and watched Kenneth massage his feet, impressed with his technique and skill. He lit the joint, relaxed and rolled over onto his stomach while Kenneth done considerable work on Ray's legs and lower back then worked his way up to his shoulders and neck. Pleased, Ray turned over onto his back so Kenneth could massage his chest, arms, abs, thighs, legs and finally with permission, Ray's big brown cock. Kenneth finished the massage with his mouth. Happily sucking Ray's cock and giving it a thorough tongue-lashing as it slid deep into his throat.

Ray looked at Kenneth sucking him then focused on his ass. Kenneth was leaning over Ray on his knees his ass pointed upwards and Ray studied it. "Virgin ass huh?" he chuckled to himself. He was getting hard and decided to fuck Kenneth. "Get me a rubber bitch!" he snapped. "Then grease yo ass."

Kenneth's heart was racing as he nervously scrambled about then quickly produced a condom. He lubed up in a hurry then offered the condom to Ray.

"You put it on me bitch!" Ray demanded. "Suck it up first...get it real hard then slide the rubber on it and spread your ass."

Kenneth sucked for all he was worth and soon slid the condom onto Ray's throbbing manhood. He then climbed onto the bed and perched on his knees.

"Aw naw...turn over on your back!" Ray ordered then pushed Kenneth's legs back against his shoulders, "Keep em there," he demanded. He pulled Kenneth's ass to the edge of the bed, stroked his hard cock then positioned the head against Kenneth's asshole. "Don't fight it bitch," Ray instructed. "You want it so stay loose...you got that?"

"Yeah...I got it! Do it...come on Ray...do me," Kenneth begged, excited and frightened with nervous anticipation. For years he had longed for this moment in hopes of satisfying that deep carnal need that lived within him.

Ray pushed hard and the head of his cock forced its way inside Kenneth's asshole. Kenneth screamed and attempted to pull away, but Ray held on to him and pushed deeper causing Kenneth to squeeze his ass muscles as tight as he could momentarily stopping Ray's penetration.

"No! Stop it hurts! Please take it out Ray...please? Please stop," Kenneth gasped.

"Shut-up and relax!" Ray demanded.

"NO! I mean it goddamnit! Take it out Ray!" Kenneth snapped.

Ray widened his stance for balance then hit Kenneth hard in the chest with his fist, knocking the wind out of him then pushing his cock in deeper when Kenneth exhaled.

"Owe...owe...stop it! Stop it Ray! Ugh...OWE! OWE! IT HURTS! Stop it! NO! Stop it goddamnit! Get your fucking black cock out of me. I fucking mean it Ray!" Kenneth howled.

"Shut up bitch and take this dick," Ray ordered as he began to slowly stroke in and out of Kenneth, who despite his protest was beginning to grind his hips.

Kenneth's ass was tight and gave ground grudgingly as Ray continued to force himself in deeper, leaving Kenneth suspended between the pain...and the thrill. Once Ray got most of his cock inside, Kenneth's ass loosened considerably so Ray began to fuck him long and deep with a good rhythm. Then taking great delight in Kenneth's mixed emotions Ray slowed his assault. He pushed his cock deep inside Kenneth then pulled it nearly all the way out several times before pushing it all the way inside and deep grinding.

Kenneth was deeply conflicted. Ray's invasion into his ass had caused incredible physical pain that slowly gave way to an intense level of pleasure that excited him like never before. He wailed and cursed at Ray while attempting to pump his ass in rhythm. Then suddenly Kenneth sucked in his breath as cum exploded from his cock, landing on his stomach, chest and chin.

"Aw yeah...you sho nuff like this dick in yo ass don't you?" Ray asked triumphantly.

Kenneth was silent.

"Come on bitch! Admit it...you just came like a motherfucker and with no help cause this dick is up yo butt...and you like that! Don't you?" Ray demanded.

"No! Get off me you black son of a bitch!" Kenneth snarled.

"Uh-huh...you want me to slam this dick up yo honkey ass I see..." Ray responded with a grin. "Well you got it son...uh-huh...I'm sho nuff gonna fuck you now." Ray leaned forward and pressed Kenneth tight to the mattress forcing his cock even deeper into Kenneth's hot virgin ass then fucked him hard. Fully excited, Ray's cock grew even larger as it rocked and pumped deep inside Kenneth for several long moments before hot cum exploded into the condom.

Kenneth was beyond incredulous and greatly relieved when Ray's big dick finally slipped out of his sore, quivering asshole. He felt violated and angry, yet sexy and vulnerable as he squirmed with the new experience of cool air rushing into his gaping asshole. After all the years of wondering, wanting and experimenting with various objects, he had actually been taken by a man. That reality still had him alternating between ecstasy and agony. He was thrilled to know that he took it, liked most of it and now understands that he truly needs to feel a man inside him, but not Ray. Definitely not Ray. Ray was rough and fucked him like he was a piece of meat. It hurt and still hurts because Ray's cock was too big. At first Kenneth thought he would pass out from the pain. It felt like his ass was being split wide open and Ray pushed in way too deep. Yet in spite of that, it had felt good too and touched something very deep inside him. Now he was no longer a virgin and he could not wait to proudly offer his ass to David's much smaller cock. He would be happy to suck Ray anytime but one fuck was enough. Kenneth started to settle into the single bed but stopped and asked, "Uh can I sleep with you tonight Ray?"

Ray threw the condom into the fireplace, washed up and climbed into bed. "Well seeing as how I done fucked you…yeah I guess you can," he responded with a wide grin.

Kenneth snuggled in and they both soon fell asleep.

The rising sun shining through the window caused Ray to wake up. He moved his head out of the sunbeam very aware of the pleasant fact that he had a major morning hard-on. He looked at Kenneth still sleeping with his naked ass all nestled up against him. Ray reached over Kenneth and picked up the lubricant. He lubed his cock then pushed it into Kenneth's ass.

Kenneth awoke instantly and struggled, but Ray pinned him to the bed and pushed deeper into him with one firm smooth stroke. Kenneth quickly collapsed in surrender while Ray's cock stretched his rectum as it began to slide in and out. Screaming and cursing Kenneth buried his face in the pillow. Yet...in spite of his expressed displeasure, he enthusiastically pumped his ass to meet Ray's thrusting cock. For several long moments they fucked in rhythm. Ray's hard cock slid smoothly back and forth, while Kenneth whimpered and cursed, overwhelmed by the cock inside him. When he felt his climax start to build, Ray long stroked Kenneth for several moments before pushing deep inside then exploding. He wasn't wearing a condom and the feel of Ray's hard cock splashing hot semen deep inside his ass caused Kenneth to cum without even being hard.

In spite of getting off, Kenneth was not happy about getting fucked again. "I didn't ask for that!" he snapped when Ray rolled off him.

"So what...you got it," Ray grinned.

"Please don't do it anymore," Kenneth pleaded. "I've had enough! I mean I really want to suck you anytime you say, but my ass has had enough...please Ray?"

Ray chuckled. "Don't think you are breaking my heart," he advised. "I didn't want to fuck you in the first place. I wanna fuck Marsha, but since you got in the way, you got fucked and I took all I wanted...and if I want some more I will take some more."

"You raped me this morning, you know that don't you?" Kenneth questioned.

"If you don't make some coffee and breakfast pronto I'm gonna rape yo ass again!" Ray shot back.

"Kenneth prepared breakfast, served Ray in bed then tided up the cabin. Occasional shivers of pleasure teased his groin making him pause and shudder while his asshole was sore and felt as if it were hanging wide open. In spite of the fact that Ray's cock had changed him forever Kenneth wanted no more of it. He was upset with Ray and wanted to leave. But after breakfast Ray sat on the porch and worked on his carving until just before noon then ordered Kenneth to prepare lunch. After eating Ray packed his bag then took a short hike through the woods while Kenneth closed up the cabin.

They began their journey home in silence because both men were quietly angry with the other. Ray was angry because he suspected Kenneth had lied about Marsha coming on the trip. The more he thought about it, the more he became convinced that Kenneth tricked him because he wanted to get fucked and have the dick all to himself. Marsha didn't even figure into it. Kenneth wanted to get fucked so he can please some other guy. Feeling a little used, Ray had Kenneth pull into a roadside rest stop. He ordered him to park far away from the other cars then pulled out his cock. "Come on son...get busy," he ordered.

Kenneth took a deep breath...he was angry and upset with Ray and did not intend to go fishing with him again. He was grateful to Ray for teaching him to deep throat a cock and he was especially grateful that Ray fucked him the first time, although he should have tried to be more gentle and understanding. The second time Ray took him was deeply satisfying but wrong, totally unforgivable and made him feel like a common slut. In spite of his feelings, Kenneth knew Ray was in charge and he also knew that he could not resist sucking Ray's big powerful cock. He leaned over and enjoyed himself for several minutes before drinking Ray's juice then getting back on the road. When Kenneth parked in front of his apartment building Ray grabbed his gear and hopped out of the Jeep.

"Can we do it again sometime?" Kenneth asked.

"Sure…call me and make sure you give my love to Marsha. Catch you later," Ray responded.

Kenneth watched Ray disappear into his apartment then gunned the jeep toward home. Neither man expected to see the other again.

Chapter seven

*M*arsha *spent Sunday afternoon* at the tennis club and arrived home after Kenneth. He had put his gear away, took a long hot bath, sent a quick email and was watching a movie when she arrived. Marsha was disappointed to find him somewhat preoccupied and just a little distant. She had hoped he would be invigorated and horny. She knew Ray was not David. Ray was secure within his sexuality, had no particular need for close male bonding and probably wasn't the best choice of a fishing and wrestling buddy for Kenneth. She suspected Ray had ignored Kenneth for most of the trip and he was sulking. Annoyed, Marsha hurried out to a civic club meeting she did not have to attend then continued to honor her schedule, which was intentionally maxed out.

Over the next three weeks Kenneth obeyed orders, but their attempts at sex were disappointments at best. Marsha was at wits end and pondered getting inside Kenneth's head, finding out about his fishing trip and where he was now. But, she knew that could only lead to inviting Ray back to their house or auditioning new playmates. She then thought about calling David or booking a short cruise but instead admitted she had simply had enough. So over the next several days Marsha researched several sex therapists and psychiatrists, picking what she felt were the best qualified then scheduling Kenneth an appointment with both. His first appointment was more than two weeks away but Marsha did not tell Kenneth about either appointment. In fact they now communicated very little. Kenneth wasn't just sulking he was distant in a strange sort of way and preoccupied. Marsha kept her schedule full, avoiding Kenneth and hoping for a miracle from his upcoming therapy.

Two days before his first appointment with the sex therapist Kenneth was still unaware that he in fact had such an appointment. Marsha had planned to tell him on the night before but Kenneth had other plans. Marsha arrived at home that evening feeling frazzled and tense. She had been uneasy and tense since her encounter with Raymond Jenkins and Kenneth's current behavior only made it worse. Marsha was beginning to think about therapy for herself but immediately picked up a strange vibe when she walked into the house. Something was different. She could feel it but could not put her finger on it until she entered their bedroom and saw a letter lying on the bed. She knew what it meant before picking it up but could not resist reading it.

Marsha,

I am sorry, really sorry. I don't know how to say this except to say it. David has left Cyndi and filed for a divorce so I must leave you to be with David. You are the one person who really knows how much I love David and I hope you will understand my need to be with him now that I have the chance. I have talked to a divorce lawyer and he will be

contacting you in a few days. I want nothing but the freedom to truly love David and I will ask for nothing in the divorce proceedings. I will always love you Marsha and thank you for the years we shared together. I'm sorry for our marriage and what we had but I know this is best for both of us. Good-bye Mother and please wish me well.
Kenneth

Marsha read the letter again then looked about the room. All of Kenneth's personal items were missing. She flung open his closet and it was empty. She was stunned, angry and strangely relieved. She paced the house, wringing her hands for the remainder of the evening before finally falling asleep with tears in her eyes. The following day she called in to work sick then called Kenneth's employer. Kenneth had resigned at the end of the previous week leaving only his attorney as a forwarding address. Marsha immediately got drunk and stayed that way all day. She cursed Kenneth, David, all men in general then busied herself destroying any photograph, likeness or reminder of Kenneth in the house.

The next day Marsha awoke and returned to work in complete denial. Successfully performing her job, keeping civic and social engagements and making appropriate excuses for Kenneth's absence. She even received a call from Kenneth's attorney, discussed the grounds for divorce and the property settlement then accepted the legal summons of divorce from the deputy sheriff at her door, all while still in denial. Marsha was unwilling and unable to admit her husband had left her for a man and steadfastly refused to discuss her situation with family, friends or even Tina.

Soon however the harsh reality of suddenly living alone began to close in and take its toll. In nearly three weeks Marsha had heard nothing from Kenneth. Nothing except through his lawyer. No good-bye, no chance to vent, to discuss or understand, no sense of closure, nothing but emptiness. Kenneth had proved to be a world class wimp, sneaking off when she wasn't looking. Not all that much to lose. But he was all she had and overall it had been a good marriage. There were problems, sure everyone has problems, but they were working on them. Marsha searched for an answer...what went wrong and when? She thought about Cyndi...she too has lost her husband to a man. Marsha picked up the phone and attempted to call Cyndi but her phone number had changed and was now unlisted.

The next day Marsha reviewed the divorce settlement and decided against hiring her own lawyer. As a legal researcher she was quite accustomed to reading legalese. The grounds were irreconcilable differences and the settlement was simple, Kenneth got the cabin, his Jeep, personal effects, clothes and most of the bills. Marsha got everything else. An uncontested divorce required only a brief appearance in court and it was all over. She signed the documents then put them aside, went to bed and cried herself to sleep. She awoke depressed but delivered the documents to Kenneth's lawyer and began using more valium to get through the day and more liquor to get through the night.

As her court date approached, Marsha was considering getting away for a while on an ocean cruise. She arrived at home with an array of travel brochures only to find a deputy sheriff waiting. He served her with a subpoena ad testificandum then left. Marsha was astounded; her divorce was only days away from being decreed, what was this all about. She stepped inside and began reading the subpoena. "Blah, blah…in the cause of Cynthia Michelle Rollins versus David Henry Rollins." This was David and Cyndi's divorce…Marsha collapsed into a chair and read the entire document. She screamed when she discovered that David had filed for divorce but Cyndi contested it and counter-filed charging adultery and naming Marsha Weber as the other woman.

Marsha threw the papers into the air then stormed around the house, stunned and angry. She fixed a strong drink, drank it quickly then fixed another. Again Marsha screamed loudly in disbelief then emptied her dresser looking for the cocaine she hid several weeks back. She collapsed into the pile of undergarments her dresser had produced, sipped her drink and wallowed in self-pity.

After the liquor kicked in she became giddy throwing her slips, panties and bras into the air until the envelope containing the cocaine suddenly fluttered into view. Marsha grabbed it then froze. Written on the outside of the envelope was the name, "Ray Jenkins" and his pager number. Marsha lightly ran her fingers over Ray's name then picked up the phone and paged him.

Ray was fixing the second round of after dinner drinks, when his pager sounded. He had just eaten a delicious dinner brought to him by a casual lady friend intent on marrying him. The lady had three school-aged children and considered Ray the perfect catch. It was an old game he despised but occasionally played to his advantage. On this night he had planned to yield a few points for the sake of answering natures call. At times Ray hated his sex drive, it forced him to compromise, take risk and make moves he otherwise would never make. He looked at the number in his pager, it was vaguely familiar but he couldn't identify it, so he waited his customary eight minutes before calling.

Ray was stunned and speechless when Marsha answered the phone. She was his legendary conquest, the lady against whom all other women were now measured. He quickly recovered and briefly talked to her then pretended to his date that the call was a work-related emergency. Since he was a maintenance man, it was an easy sell and he quickly sent his company on her way then headed to Marsha's house.

Marsha collapsed into his arms when Ray stepped through her front door. They settled onto the sofa and he spent more than an hour comforting, consoling, kissing and caressing her while she sobbed and poured out her troubles. Marsha felt snug and secure in Ray's arms...she looked up at him and suddenly was on fire. All her pent up passion, lust, need and desire broke loose in a flood. Ray was at first overwhelmed by the intensity of her sudden romantic attack but it struck deep, unleashing his own pent up passions. Their kisses became liquid as they melted together entering that rarefied air reserved only for those few fortunate people that actually find their true soul mate.

Marsha held Ray's face in her hands and beamed at him. For the first time in her adult life, real peace and true serenity flooded through her. Nothing else mattered except this man. In a strange way she felt he was part of her and at that instant she knew Ray would be her next husband and lifetime partner. She tore open his shirt then lovingly kissed his chest and stomach. She laughed, helped him undress, then twirled around and done her best strip tease, thoroughly enjoying her today because she knew it would still be there tomorrow.

Ray was struggling to keep up. It all seemed too good to be true. Kenneth was history and Marsha was now dancing nude for him. His cock grew hard and throbbed as he watched her. She was a gorgeous woman; feminine, classy, soft, sweet and has a brain. Ray knew he could fall in love with this woman...in fact that was already happening. He scooped her up and carried her to the bedroom. Wrapped in each other's arms they eased onto the bed, both thrilled to finally have unrestricted access to the other.

Marsha and Ray were beyond simple lust or just sexual desire. Their need for each other was rooted in a shared feeling for a special love they both had wished for but never really expected to share. For several moments they lay motionless, gazing deeply into each others eyes before their lips met in a gentle kiss. Another kiss, then another as the kisses grew hotter then wet then demanding. The air was electric when Ray entered Marsha. Jolts of pure delight soared through both of them and they cried out in unison, each excited and thrilled by the others touch. Their unbridled passions took them to new heights. A completely new and exhilarating level of thrill, love and satisfaction. It was only exhaustion that finally overcame their glorious sexual marathon. Late that night, totally spent and pressed tightly together they drifted into sound peaceful sleep.

When the alarm clock sounded, Marsha shut it off then picked up the phone and called into work sick. When she hung up, Ray took the phone and called in sick on his job, then reached for Marsha but she ducked under the sheet and began fondling his quickly rising manhood.

Ray was still overwhelmed by his sudden good fortune. He looked at the sheet bobbing up and down over Marsha's head and smiled. Oddly enough he had instantly fallen in love with this woman and somehow he now knew she would become his wife. Ray threw off the sheet, repositioned himself and began kissing the inside of her thighs. In no time they were locked in an extremely intense sixty-nine, which left them trembling with true erotic fulfillment.

Marsha and Ray spent the remainder of that day and most of the following weekend in bed together. They had a lot of sex and almost non-stop conversation. The mind is the driving force behind sex so their soulful meeting of the minds produced three special days in their lives that neither could really describe nor ever forget. They couldn't hide their feelings from each other and didn't try, as their compatibility was nothing short of remarkable. Both felt like they had known the other most of their lives. They were friends, liked each other as people, adored each other sexually and had already ventured far beyond infatuation or admiration. They had truly fallen deeply in love. Much to their credit Ray and Marsha faced themselves and each other squarely, spoke honestly and by Monday morning had committed to a serious relationship.

They agreed to give each other space but were inseparable. If Ray did not spend the night at Marsha's place she spent the night at his. They were an instant couple from day one.

Ray accompanied Marsha to her divorce proceedings holding her hand throughout while Kenneth crouched between his lawyers. Before Ray re-entered her life Marsha had longed to vigorously confront Kenneth, now she cared less. She glanced at him several times but wasn't bothered by his refusal to even look in her direction. He hurried in and out of the courtroom nestled between his lawyers, glanced quickly at Marsha one time and never saw Ray Jenkins. The proceeding was brief and for Ray a happy occasion. Afterward he took Marsha to an elegant restaurant then to a comedy club before retiring to his place and making sweet love to her.

Marsha lay awake late into that night pleased and excited. She found it hard to believe that with the stroke of a judge's pen, she was completely free of Kenneth and his sexual quirk. She was a divorcee…single again with a new man in her life. And that man made all the difference. She smiled at Ray who was peacefully sleeping. Marsha couldn't stand the thought of being without him, even for one night. She badly wanted him to give up his apartment and move in with her, but didn't want to pressure him. She glanced around the room and smiled even broader. Life with Kenneth had totally vanished, almost as if it had never existed. Now there was Ray, a real man that satisfied and excited her. Sex didn't really happen for Marsha until she slept with Ray. His masculine charm and big hard cock touched unreached places within her, taking her to heights of intense pleasure she hadn't known were possible. As far as she was concerned she was a true virgin when Ray took her for the first time because everything before him had been child's play. Now no matter what, she was determined to become his wife and knew she eventually would. She snuggled close, lightly kissed him and went to sleep, contented in that special way only true lovers can be.

A few weeks later, Ray drove Marsha to a courthouse in the Northeast corner of the state. She was required by subpoena to testify at David and Cyndi's divorce proceeding and not happy about it. They arrived early and ran into David in the parking lot. Accompanied by his lawyer, he stopped only to say hello and ask if they would give him a ride to the airport after the court proceedings, then hurried off.

When Marsha checked in with the clerk of the court, she and Ray were shown to a small witness room where they sat alone holding hands until Marsha was called into court. She was directed to the witness stand, sworn to tell the truth, asked to state her full name then told to be seated.

As soon as she sat down, Cyndi's lawyer leapt to his feet. "Mrs. Weber in May of last year did you accompany your husband at that time to a cabin in Southern Michigan," he asked.

"Yes I did," Marsha responded.

"How long did you stay in this cabin?" the lawyer questioned.

"Uh…we arrived Friday evening and left Sunday afternoon," Marsha replied.

"Did Mr. David Rollings also stay at the cabin that weekend?" the lawyer inquired.

"Yes," Marsha confirmed.

"Did you have sex with Mr. Rollings during that stay?" the lawyer questioned.

"It wasn't like that...I mean..." Marsha attempted to explain.

"Just answer the question Mrs. Weber did you or did you not have sexual intercourse with Mr. David Rollings during your weekend stay at that cabin? Yes or no?" the lawyer demanded.

"Ye...yes...but..." Marsha stammered.

"Thank you Mrs. Weber, I have no further questions of this witness your honor," the lawyer concluded.

"Mr. Davenport!" the judge barked.

"Uh...uh...no questions your honor...uh we have no questions for this witness," Attorney Davenport responded.

"Then the witness is released without subject to recall. Thank you Mrs. Weber you are excused," the judge concluded.

"But...no please let me explain...it wasn't like that at all," Marsha protested.

"That won't be necessary Mrs. Weber you may step down," the judge instructed.

"That's not fair you should at least want to hear the truth about it!" Marsha insisted.

"Mrs. Weber you are free to go...and if you don't go...it is going to cost you a lot of money at the very least," the judge advised.

Marsha stepped from the witness chair then defiantly marched from the courtroom. Once back inside the witness room she collapsed into Ray's comforting arms. He consoled and helped her vent then compose herself before they left the building and waited in their car for David.

Marsha was hurting and angry, "I can not believe it Ray! I just fucking cannot believe it! Those assholes! Now I'll forever be a scarlet woman! God! What assholes!" she fumed. Marsha continued to vent for several minutes until Ray suddenly kissed her deeply for several moments.

"You know what pumpkin?" he gasped after breaking the kiss.

"What?" Marsha asked.

"You oughta march right back into that courtroom and slap the shit outta that judge...get both them lawyers too!" Ray suggested.

Marsha first giggled then broke into laughter. Ray laughed and she hugged him tight. They both liked to hug and laugh. They liked the feeling of their laughing bodies shaking together. "Look at me..." Marsha giggled, "I've just suffered the most humiliating experience of my life and twenty minutes later here I am happy, I'm laughing ha-ha-ha...and what happened in that courtroom really doesn't matter. All thanks to you Ray Jenkins...you're everything to me and I love you. I could not have survived this ordeal without you. Sometimes I think..."

"Whoa! Hold up!" Ray put in. "Go back to that I love you part, I haven't heard that before."

"Oh god! I'm sorry Ray...I promised myself I wouldn't say that," Marsha replied.

"Really? Why?" Ray asked.

"Because those three little words may put pressure on you and I don't want to do that," Marsha replied.

"Even if you feel that way?" Ray questioned.

"Unfortunately yes," Marsha admitted.

"Hum...do you really feel that way?" Ray asked.

"Yes!" Marsha confessed. "I love you Ray...and I'm in love with you."

"Well then we even pumpkin...cause the truth is I fell in love with you the first time we met...and since we have been together I've grown to love you more than anyone I've ever known...Mama included!" Ray declared, then stroked Marsha's face and gazed deeply into her eyes. "Marsha?" he softly spoke.

"Yes Ray," Marsha responded.

"I love you Marsha!" Ray admitted.

"I love you Ray and I am really thrilled to know you love me too."

"Marsha?" Ray began anew.

"Yes sweetheart?" Marsha responded as her heart began to beat faster.

"Marsha? Will you marry me?" Ray asked.

"YES!!! Oh yes...yes...yes! Oh Ray! I love you so much...YES I'LL MARRY YOU!" Marsha loudly declared.

"Ut oh...I think I asked the wrong question," Ray teased.

"No you didn't! And I accepted," Marsha beamed. "We are now officially engaged and I am the happiest woman alive...YES!"

Ray chuckled and held Marsha tight; neither of them had ever been happier and was concluding another wet kiss when David knocked on the window of the car.

After putting his travel case into the trunk, David climbed into the back seat and began asking Ray a series of legal questions. Then was surprised and happy to learn that Ray was not Marsha's lawyer but her fiancée and the same man that had twice defeated Kenneth on the wrestling mat. He winked and smiled at Ray while thanking him for the ride. In spite of the bitter, unhappy legal battle inside the courtroom, David was upbeat and anxious to return to his new life. He gave Marsha his address and phone number, then told her that he and Kenneth had moved to San Francisco and were living together as an openly gay couple. Both being computer programmers they had quickly found work and were doing quite well. As the car entered the airport, David thanked Marsha for destroying the inhibitions and self imposed barriers between he and Kenneth. She had done what they never could. She liberated them then forced them to become honest men for the first time in their lives. He went on to thank Ray for paving the way, then hopped out of the car, retrieved his travel case and disappeared into the terminal.

Ray pointed the car toward the interstate highway while Marsha reclined in her seat, deep in thought. "I can't believe David just thanked me," she sighed. "I never really had anything with Kenneth; he belonged to David long before I met him. And I certainly wasn't trying to liberate them...I was angry and hurt. I wanted to punish and humiliate them. I don't know...I can't believe that one weekend has caused so many repercussions. Now not only am I a scarlet woman, I'm also the liberator of the gay spirit," she pouted.

"I think you're being way too hard on yourself pumpkin," Ray responded.

"No, its true Ray...every bit of it is true," Marsha admitted. "Kenneth and David were hiding behind a wrestling game and I exposed them. I had sex with David and made Kenneth watch, then I forced them into real intimacy with each other. I even made them openly kiss and fondle each other. Funny huh...I thought they would be repulsed by it. But...what did I know? I was following the advice of a girlfriend and at the time I thought it worked. But...as we now know they were already in love and just needed me to make them face up to it. Still I don't regret it, even though Kenneth left me, Cyndi publicly embarrassed me and now David actually thanked me for it...I don't know. Maybe you're right he thanked you too. It's possible he's just stressed out by the divorce."

"Don't be to sure, I spent a weekend at that cabin with Kenneth too," Ray replied.

"Oh my god! That's right..." Marsha gasped. "I almost forgot...and Kenneth was acting different after that trip. Oh no Ray, you didn't?"

"Yep...fraid I did," Ray admitted.

"RAY? No...Ray how could you?" Marsha asked in astonishment.

"I was angry and felt cheated," Ray responded.

"Angry...cheated?" Marsha questioned.

"Yeah...I figured Kenneth lied about you coming on the trip with us and I thought that meant I wasn't ever going to see you again so I tried to make Kenneth pay for deceiving me," Ray explained.

"Wait...Kenneth understood very clearly that I was not going on that fishing trip so why were you expecting me?" Marsha asked.

"Because the lying shithead said you were going when he called," Ray replied. "And when he picked me up he said you were working on some important shit that had to be in court soon and were going to drive up later. And get this...he said you would page ME if you couldn't make it or had a problem. Then Saturday morning he called you from a pay phone and said you were still working but hope to make it up before nightfall, course if you didn't you wasn't coming. It was about then that I figured you never were coming on this trip in the first place. Then just a little later Kenneth started begging me to bump his butt. The truth is at first I told him no, I really didn't want to, that ain't my thing. But he kept begging and when I found out he had never had it before, I decided it was a perfect way to punish the hell out of him for tricking me."

"Did he like it?" Marsha asked.

"Don't think so," Ray responded. "But then I really don't know. He screamed like hell, begged me to stop and called me every foul name in the book, but he didn't really fight it and even tried to get with the rhythm a little, so I think he was kinda grateful. He had told me he wanted to get drilled, that's what he called it, so he could please some old friend that really wanted him but refused to if it hurt him. So yeah I guess he was grateful, but not real happy with the experience...he begged me not to do it again."

"You took him by force?" Marsha questioned.

"Naw, I took him with malice," Ray responded. "I knew it hurt him. I knew he really wanted me to stop...but I also knew that he tricked me into being there for that very reason. I was pretty damn sure I would never see you again...so I took great pleasure in showing him no mercy."

"So that's what David meant when he thanked you for paving the way?" Marsha replied.

"Yeah I guess so," Ray agreed.

"Ray..." Marsha began after a long silence.

"Yeah pumpkin," Ray replied.

"Do you realize we conspired without even knowing it to get Kenneth and David together?" Marsha commented. "I took away their masks and you made Kenneth accept the fact he is more woman than man."

"Hum…only true soulmates can pull that off…that's really cool…less you mad at me pumpkin?" Ray responded.

"Mad? No. I'll tell you what I am. I am soon to be Mrs. Raymond Jenkins. Whatever it took or whatever it takes to make that happen is well worth it. You are everything to me and I love you Ray…more than anyone ever. So I don't care about yesterday. I'm only concerned about my today and tomorrow's with you."

Ray eased the car off the road pulled Marsha into his arms, then whispered into her ear. "Thank you lord for this precious woman and for allowing me to finally experience, understand and share true and lasting love. I promise to cherish and love this beautiful creature with every fiber of my being for as long as I am alive. I love you for this lord and I won't let you down… amen."

Her heart pounded and tears trickled down Marsha's face as she held tight to Ray, "Take me home sweetheart," she whispered. "Please…I love you so much…take me to our bed."

"And to our future," Ray responded as he steered the car back onto the highway and quickly drove the remaining distance to Marsha's house with her snuggled next to him, resting her head on his shoulder, kissing his neck, massaging his chest and whispering sweet nothings.

Chapter eight

*T*he next few weeks went by in a blur as Ray and Marsha began to put the pieces of their commitment and future into place. First Ray moved from his apartment to Marsha's house. Neither regretted it but both of them quickly became aware that the house was not a comfortable fit. The ghost of Kenneth, the attitudes of some neighbors and a mutual desire to create their own special love nest spurred Marsha to put the house up for sale. They shared mutual visions and decided that owning a house created burdens they rather not have. So Marsha and Ray began shopping for the perfect condominium.

After she and Ray set a date, Marsha was swept away with her new romance, deeply in love and began to plan a large festive wedding. But much to their surprise and disgust, their announced wedding plans drew many negative and unkind remarks from both families and friends. Ray's daughter broke her self-imposed silence by threatening to disown Ray and vowed never to let him see his yet to be conceived grandchild. His sister pronounced him to be an "ole fool" and insisted she would have nothing to do with neither Ray nor his "white wife!" Ray's brother was certain Ray had pretty much lost his mind but agreed to be best man...if nobody else could be found for the job. Ray's mom however was quite pleased to know her son was getting married and that she had a wedding to attend, during which she would have a grand measure of importance.

Marsha also suffered. The attitudes at work changed when she replaced Kenneth picture with Ray's in the little frame on her desk. When she found it had been scribbled on, she placed it in her desk drawer which she kept open when at her desk and locked while away. Her family was a larger disappointment and she was stunned. In spite of the fact that as a child she had been taught to be tolerant and open to all people. To judge only by the individual, not their race, color, religion or anything else, her father now insisted she was selling herself short and angrily refused to attend the wedding. Her mother was sure Marsha was acting in haste, while really heartbroken over the loss of Kenneth. Only Marsha's brother Michael was upbeat and encouraging. He liked Ray and they quickly became good friends and football watching buddies. Marsha was delighted; her brother had never felt comfortable around Kenneth and never really liked him. Michael and his wife were soon to become Ray and Marsha's only real friends.

As days passed into weeks, the wide circle of friends Ray and Marsha had individually known began to shun and avoid them; a few even made slurs or hurtful remarks. Marsha and Ray soon found themselves all alone but enjoying their solitude. The rejection of family and friends forced them into isolation which made their love grow stronger and become even more meaningful. They really became true best friends; completely enjoyed each others company and soon preferred to be alone together.

Very aware of their limited social acceptance, Ray and Marsha narrowed their condominium search down to three then decided to have a small intimate wedding ceremony and fly off to a fabulous honeymoon the day after.

Marsha was happily preparing dinner when yet another sheriff's deputy rang her doorbell and served her with yet another subpoena. She was speechless and stunned, accepted the subpoena, closed the door, sat down on the sofa and read it, her blood slowly beginning to boil as she read. Cynthia Rollins had successfully sued David for divorce on the grounds of adultery by naming Marsha as the other woman. Now Cyndi and her children were suing the other woman for alienation of affection, loss of parental support, loss of conjugal rights and so on. Marsha was furious beyond belief, causing Ray to spend considerable time attempting to calm and console her before finally directing her angry energy to a freaky sexual encounter.

It was a rare experience for both of them as they got down and dirty. Ray became demanding and dominating. He ordered Marsha about and she meekly complied. Marsha purposely displeased Ray and he made her lay across his lap then proceeded to slap her ass hard…until it glowed nice and pink. She gasped and wiggled, her flesh tingling as waves of pure delight ripped through her. Ray ordered her to her knees, then taunted her with his hard-on before allowing her to touch, taste, suck and enjoy it. She devoured him completely, taking his breath away and herself to a new level. Marsha seized the moment and ordered Ray onto his back then climbed astride him and slowly worked his hard cock deep inside her. She placed her hands firmly against his shoulders and looked deep into his eyes while they made love with rhythm and passion. Truly in love, they kissed, caressed, soared in mutual explosions then basked and snuggled in the warm and fuzzy afterglow.

Although she did not hire a lawyer for her divorce Marsha immediately hired a well known lawyer to fight this legal action and he took Cyndi's lawsuit very seriously. The lawyer unsuccessfully attempted to have the lawsuit thrown out as frivolous then pushed for an early court date, while advising Marsha to freeze her assets and plans. He also advised that the key witness was David. The honest description of his daily life would clearly establish exactly whom he left Cyndi for. David lived with Kenneth while Marsha lives with and is waiting for the cloud over her head to lift so she can marry Raymond Jenkins. With David's testimony the case was a no-brainer without it another story. David could be subpoenaed but the subpoena actually meant little in another state.

At first Marsha was reluctant because she wasn't comfortable calling David. She still had the phone number he had given her but it had been months since she had seen or talked to him. She stalled the lawyer and hurried home to talk it over with Ray. Two hours later, Ray called David and he quickly agreed to fly back and testify on Marsha's behalf. He even insisted on paying his own airfare. Meanwhile, no attempt at any settlement was offered and a few months later the lawsuit went to trial.

Ray drove Marsha to the same little courthouse in the northeast corner of the state. Cyndi was smug and glared at them when they walked in. She turned completely white however when David entered the courtroom. Marsha and Ray had picked David up at the airport and brought him to the courthouse. He stopped in the men's room to freshen up and entered the courtroom a few minutes behind Ray, Marsha and her lawyer. He took a seat then casually looked around the room. When he spotted Cyndi, David smiled and waved real big but she turned her head and refused to look at him again.

David's blunt and open testimony declaring his long time and continuing love for Kenneth brought the proceedings to a quick halt. Judgment for the defendant...the lawsuit was dismissed. Cyndi ran from the courtroom while Marsha and Ray took their time then treated David to prime rib at his favorite local restaurant before taking him back to the airport.

David was excited and all abuzz from the moment he arrived. He talked nonstop throughout dinner and during the trip from and to the airport. He was excited because he and Kenneth had worked their jobs for less than four months before starting their own software designing business and finding themselves in the right place at the right time. They were successful beyond their wildest imagination. A few months back they bought a two hundred and seventy-three acre ranch at the northern tip of the wine country. Close to San Francisco, yet far away. He and Kenneth truly love the wonderful open space and freedom from the petty hassles of the city. They love it and it is a perfect place, but they have a problem.

David sighed and leaned back in his seat. "The ranch is run down and scruffy," he admitted. "We bought it from an estate and it has been unoccupied for a long time, so nothing is growing on it except weeds and brush. It has a real nice ranch house on the south end of it and an old farmhouse on the east edge. Both houses are in good shape but they are too big for us so Kenneth and I had a really cool A-Frame cabin built on the north end. The rest of the ranch is just empty. It doesn't bother Kenny, he planted lots of really pretty flowers around our new A-Frame and just loves the place. But it bothers me because I know the ranch could turn a profit or at the very least break even. It needs a foreman...somebody to take charge and bring that land to life. I sure as hell don't know how to fix things or manage physical stuff. I'm not qualified and don't want to be a ranch foreman. Neither is Kenny and he isn't interested anyway. We need someone...someone we can trust...and I'm not talking employees here. I'm talking a piece of the action," David offered.

"How big a piece?" Ray questioned.

"A nice percentage of the Ranch, but you gotta come see it at least!" David replied.

"Only one man at a time can conduct an orchestra, preach a sermon or run the show...do you get my drift?" Ray quizzed.

"Yes sir! Loud and clear!" David beamed. "I'm offering total control and authority on all acres of the ranch, with the exception of the clearly marked one acre on which Kenny and I live."

"You willing to put that in writing?" Ray asked.

"RAY?" Marsha put in.

"Yeah baby? Getting carried away huh?" Ray grinned.

Marsha smiled. "David's imagination is most likely bigger than his reality," she suggested.

"NO! I SWEAR! WE NAMED IT THE KD Ranch!" David insisted. "Just come visit. I BEG YOU! The ranch needs you guys, it really does. Just fly out and visit, then you'll see it's perfect and there are two nice houses all the way on the other side of the property standing empty, and yeah Ray I'll put that in writing...how bout twelve percent?"

"Ha..." Ray chuckled. "Food for thought my friend... food for thought."

"Oh please, do more that just think about it guys? Okay? Please? Just fly out and visit...please? I'll buy the tickets," David pleaded.

"If we decide to fly out and visit we will buy our own tickets and twelve percent sounds kinda low to me," Ray replied.

"Damn...I gotta run to catch my plane," David observed. "Come visit and we will talk...please...love you guys...bye!" David hopped from the car and hurried into the terminal.

Marsha and Ray returned home to face a serious buyer for the house with no decision made on a condo and a scheduled week of vacation coming up for both of them. Marsha accepted the offer for her house then over the next two weeks, she and Ray really tried hard to make a final decision on a condo. But nothing seemed to feel completely right. By the beginning of the third week they were weary of their housing search and made plans for their coming vacation.

On the first day of their vacation Marsha and Ray flew to Las Vegas, checked into a luxury suite then strolled hand in hand along the strip. On their second day they had breakfast in their room then took a short limo ride to a well-known Las Vegas Wedding Chapel. Their wedding ceremony was brief but elegant and very moving. They left the chapel as happy newlyweds and spent the remainder of that day consummating their marriage. They relaxed and honeymooned for another day then flew to San Francisco, rented a car and drove to the wine country of California. Destination the KD Ranch.

The KD Ranch was more in the onion and lettuce country than wine country, yet Marsha and Ray were intoxicated by the air and thrilled by the open space. They followed David's directions and arrived at the ranch in mid-afternoon. David was overjoyed to see them, while Kenneth was extremely reticent. He briefly spoke then disappeared into the A-Frame cabin. Kenneth had never forgiven Ray Jenkins for their second encounter and he was still very intimidated by Marsha.

David was excited and happily took Marsha and Ray on the grand tour of the mostly empty ranch. There were acres of overgrown land, pastures and some wooded areas. The old farmhouse like the barn had been neglected but could be restored to a wonderful cozy home. David briefly interrupted the tour by taking Marsha and Ray back to their car then requested they follow him the rest of the way. He led them all the way across the ranch to a Spanish style; stone ranch house that needed minor attention and cleaning but otherwise was in first class condition. It had a big foyer, a living room, dining room, kitchen, three bedrooms, two and a half baths and a full basement with another bathroom. There were three fireplaces, one in the living room, basement and the master bedroom.

Marsha and Ray were closely inspecting the ranch house when David chose to make his exit. He tossed them the keys, invited them to stay a few days to explore the ranch and its possibilities then hopped into his BMW and drove off. Marsha and Ray were impressed. The ranch house was very comfortable and they instantly liked it. They took their time checking it out then investigated the old farmhouse and the rest of the ranch. They chatted with a neighboring rancher, looked around the nearby town, bought groceries and cleaning supplies then settled into the ranch house.

Two days later Marsha and Ray struck a deal with David. In exchange for managing and overseeing two hundred and seventy acres of the KD Ranch, Ray and Marsha received complete ownership of the ranch house and the two acres surrounding it. They also received twenty-percent ownership of the KD Ranch while paying no expenses of operation. Should the ranch produce an income, they were to be compensated by twenty percent of any and all net profits.

It was a simple deal requiring only minimal legal work so Marsha prepared the documents, which impressed the San Francisco law firm hired to handle the transaction. She made it known she was relocating and looking for work as a legal researcher then provided a resume and impeccable references. The law firm responded with a handsome offer. It was a position Marsha could not resist because the job could be done from home by computer.

On their flight home Marsha and Ray said very little to each other. They sat looking dreamily into the others eyes and softly smiling. Communicating at a level that required no words. Upon their return, they immediately resigned their jobs and closed the sale of Marsha's house. The following week they shipped their furniture, belongings and Marsha's Toyota to the KD Ranch. After saying good bye to friends and family, Marsha and Ray settled into Ray's Town Car and spent nearly two weeks on the road leisurely driving to California. When they arrived at the ranch house they slipped into their new life on the KD Ranch as easily as putting on old shoes.

Living on opposite ends of the ranch meant the nearby town was closer to them than Kenneth and David. They were completely isolated and loved it. Days passed into weeks and Marsha easily adjusted to working at home. They transformed one of the bedrooms into Marsha's office. It was a room she loved and they took great care in the decorating, making certain her business equipment was state of the art.

Ray quickly leased grazing and growing rights on many of the acres to a neighboring rancher. The rancher badly needed more land, but did not care for David or Kenneth and would not have talked to them even if they had approached him. He liked Ray and provided a small crew of ranch hands to help clear the land. Two mornings of each week Ray attended classes on land management and ranching fundamentals at the local community college. He created a master plan for the KD ranch, made friends and joined the Tri-County Ranchers Association. He spent the remainder of his time supervising the land clearing then repairing and restoring the whole ranch, one section at a time. Occasionally he worked on the old farmhouse. It was a project Marsha also enjoyed so they spent many happy hours working, flirting and making love in the cozy old house. About ten months after Ray arrived; the ranch actually began to look like a ranch. The brush and overgrowth was gone, fields were planted and fences were repaired, some even painted. The stable behind the old farmhouse had been repaired and painted and Ray was hard at work putting a hot tub into the deck of the ranch house. He and Marsha had not seen Kenneth at all and David only twice since they arrived and were surprised when he called asking if he could come by.

David arrived shortly after dinner, pale and visibly shaken. Cyndi had recently filed suit against Kenneth for the same charges she filed against Marsha. Since she had filed out of state it really didn't mean a lot at the moment but as soon as she wises up and files in California, it means everything. David was truly worried; he knew his testimony during Marsha's lawsuit would sink Kenneth. Cyndi was a real threat to their financial well being and ownership of the ranch. Over coffee and snacks, the three of them talked offers, strategy, buy-offs, and counterattacks to defeat and defuse Cyndi's lawsuits until late in the evening.

Two days later Marsha placed a call to Cyndi. She was curt and brief but a week and three phone calls later Cyndi began to loosen up. She relaxed as their chat turned to girl things then on to real talk and shared experiences. She talked to Marsha for over an hour during the next two phone calls so Marsha suggested a visit. Cyndi made no promises except to talk and that was good enough for Marsha. She was certain something could be worked out face-to-face so three days later Ray and Marsha boarded a plane for the Midwest.

They arrived at Cyndi's house shortly after dinner. Marsha wanted to chat and make plans to do lunch the next day but Cyndi was distant and aloof, inviting them in only for a short visit. Ray occupied himself with Cyndi's two children, Kevin and Katelynn. In short order they were best friends, loudly playing and laughing. Cyndi was completely distracted and stared in awe. Both her children were very shy and reserved. Unabated laughter was not something she was used to hearing from either of them. For several minutes Cyndi and Marsha sat silently and watched Ray entertain the kids. Noticing their silence, Ray suggested taking the kids to the video arcade in the nearby mall tomorrow. Cyndi quickly said no, but Kevin and Katelynn jointly begged non-stop for permission. Marsha suggested they all make a day of it at the mall and Cyndi very reluctantly agreed. She was surprised by her kids, suspicious of Marsha and didn't quite know what to make of Ray.

When they entered the mall the next afternoon Ray and the kids headed straight for the video arcade, leaving Cyndi feeling quite lost and alone. It was rare indeed for her kids not to be within arms reach. Cynthia Rollins had not worked outside of her home since her first child was born and still didn't. Her children had never been in daycare and except for grandma every once in a while, never had a babysitter. She watched them disappear into the arcade and thought about how hard it will be to watch both of them leave home every day when Katelynn starts kindergarten in the fall. Katelynn was two years behind Kevin and too soon it seemed the nest would be empty.

Marsha interrupted her thoughts, tugging her toward a beauty salon. Marsha waived her platinum visa and despite her protest, Cyndi found herself getting a complete body service. Pedicure, manicure, facial, face and neck massage, shampoo, cut, style, polish, make-up and a take-a-long bag of beauty products. At first she was edgy and unsure but after a few minutes of being pampered gave in to its pleasure and enjoyed the experience. Cyndi was admiring herself in a large mirror when Marsha finished her final treatment and paid the bill. She accepted Cyndi's thanks but would not let her pay or make any obligation to reciprocate.

The two women went back to the arcade and for several minutes quietly watched Ray, Kevin and Katelynn, happily drive video racers. Finally they crossed the room and said hello but after a quick "Hi mommy", Kevin and Katelynn only wanted her to look at them drive. She felt a funny twinge when they said, "Uncle Ray taught us how."

Marsha tugged Cyndi out of the arcade then in and out of several stores. For a time they had real fun, trying on outrageous things, sexy things, fun things, even buying a nice sporty outfit Marsha literally demanded Cyndi keep on. Marsha also bought a sexy casual house dress Cyndi fell in love with but refused to buy and insisted Marsha not buy it for her. They peeked into the arcade only to find Uncle Ray and the kids still whooping it up, so Cyndi followed Marsha to a cappuccino bar. At first Cyndi pretended she knew what she wanted but soon admitted she was a stay at home mom and had never been in a cappuccino bar.

"It's just flavored coffee," Marsha advised. "Lots and lots of different flavored coffees and creams and spices...they are the best...do you like dark chocolate?"

"Oh I love chocolate!" Cyndi replied.

"Great!" Marsha responded. "You are gonna love this, it's my favorite."

They sat at a small table really enjoying their coffee in silence and watching people pass by until Marsha noticed Cyndi was tearing up.

"Oh please...the coffee is not that bad is it?" Marsha asked.

"No," Cyndi replied. "No really...this is the best coffee I have ever tasted...I love it...it's just that I don't understand you. You are being so nice, it makes me feel like shit for what I did to you!" she explained.

"Would you believe I understand why you did what you did?" Marsha asked.

"No you can't possibly!" Cyndi protested.

"My husband left me for a man too you know," Marsha advised.

"I'm sorry...I never..." Cyndi stammered.

"No don't apologize Cyndi...please," Marsha insisted. "Nothing can be more difficult for a woman than to lose her husband to a man. I know it's the worse...and you got kids that will never stop asking questions. So I understand you bravely tried to save face by taking me to court. You got a decree of adultery that named a woman then properly followed that up with civil action."

"Yes I did. But you kicked my behind in civil court. I had no idea where David really was and I sure didn't think you could find him. Oh god...I really feel like a piece of shit! How can you be so nice...buying me these clothes and that beauty treatment?" Cyndi questioned while tearing up again.

"Hey don't you dare mess up that expensive face! Mess it up with a real guy not over an impostor," Marsha ordered.

Cyndi giggled and dabbed lightly at her eyes. "I couldn't be as good as you. If you had done that to me and then came to my house I'd rip your face off," she admitted.

"Come on Cyndi! None of this was our fault," Marsha insisted. "We only made one honest mistake and that was the guy we fell in love with and married. One bad decision as a young woman should not ruin your entire life."

"I see you quickly made another decision!" Cyndi responded.

"The best decision I ever made in my life," Marsha blushed. "I went from hell to heaven!"

"That I find hard to believe...no guy is that good," Cyndi responded.

"Ray is...he's better than good. He's kinda like the next level...you know what I mean?" Marsha smiled.

"No...as a matter of fact I don't," Cyndi dryly replied.

"I really hope someday you will...and I mean that," Marsha replied.

Cyndi looked at her watch.

"Think it's time we drag them out of the arcade?" Marsha asked.

"Yeah...I can't believe they have been in there for almost three hours," Cyndi replied.

"They must be starving. Let's round them up and have dinner at the buffet restaurant on the other side of the mall," Marsha suggested.

"Sounds like a plan," Cyndi agreed.

When Cyndi sat down at the dinner table, Ray looked at her real hard. "Damn! You look good!" he grinned. "And you my dear look absolutely gorgeous," he winked at Marsha.

Cyndi blushed hard and Marsha smiled deep. Marsha smiled mostly because she finally put the last piece into place. She came here with a generic offer for Cyndi to drop the lawsuit but did not really have a plan or means to make it irresistible and mutually beneficial until this moment. The last piece fit perfectly, now the entire scenario was complete. Marsha chatted with Kevin and Katelynn throughout dinner, leaving Ray to chat with Cyndi. She scored big points with her napkin puppets and before dinner was over she had became Aunt Marsha.

Marsha performed one more puppet encore for Kevin and Katelynn after taking them home, then asked Cyndi if she could take them to the zoo and a popular children's movie the next day. While the children begged for permission, Marsha went on to explain to Cyndi that allowing her to take the kids for a few hours would give Ray time to explain the legal issues and offers she needed to consider.

Cyndi was overwhelmed by the whole day. She looked at her kids clinging to Uncle Ray while begging to spend a day with their newly discovered Aunt Marsha. Despite herself she liked and admired Marsha who was starting to seem like the big sister Cyndi had always longed for. Deep inside Cyndi could feel her world changing. She looked at Ray and he smiled and winked. She looked into his eyes and felt her cheeks start to glow...then quickly looked away and told Marsha the kids could go but only for a short while.

On the ride to their motel Ray chuckled, "Tell me something pumpkin?" he asked.

"What's that sweetheart?" Marsha responded.

"When did I get admitted to the bar?"

"It's perfect Ray, absolutely perfect!" Marsha replied with enthusiasm.

"Damn! I'm sure glad to know that," Ray teased. "Now if I only knew what was perfect?"

"The offer you are going to make to Cyndi sweetie," Marsha responded. "And you are going to have to call David. His offer of ten percent of net profits from the ranch until the children has finished school and/or unless she remarries is completely off base."

"It is?"

"Absolutely! Ray do you realize we have been restoring that old farmhouse for a family. This family! Cyndi is a mom with two great kids. She cooks, bakes, sews, nurses, teaches and brings something really special to a house. She is entitled to that house and a piece of the ranch, plus she really likes you."

"You may have a point about the ranch but what has liking me got to do with it?" Ray questioned.

"You like her don't you?"

"What you getting at pumpkin?"

"Okay...this is not gonna be easy to say because I really don't want you to get the wrong impression," Marsha explained. "I love you more than anyone on earth Ray Jenkins. I know we will always be together and I would die before I ever said no to you...but I wouldn't mind a little help every so often...especially now."

"What! A little help? What are you saying?" Ray questioned.

"Only that there are times when you wear me completely out sweetie...I thought I was over sexed until I met you. I'm not complaining by any means Ray. I truly and totally love you and that will never change, but honey...I am the only woman on the entire ranch," Marsha exclaimed. "It would be perfect if Cyndi lived there in the old farmhouse. The kids would have a wonderful place to play and our child will not grow up without cousins and playmates. I'd have a sister nearby and there is enough of you Mr. Jenkins for both of us."

"Damn! I didn't know I was such a bad dude!" Ray grinned.

"Ray...I really love you," Marsha sighed.

"What makes you so sure Cyndi is ready to jump my bones?" Ray asked.

"Ray...sweetie...women know these things. I knew at dinner," Marsha advised. "You don't realize it but you spent more play time with those kids in one afternoon than their father did in their entire lives."

"That's why you set me up to play lawyer tomorrow?" Ray concluded.

"Exactly! You can talk her into it... I can't!"

"And you want me to hang out alone with her knowing she wants to jump my bones," Ray questioned.

"I expect you to sleep with her," Marsha responded. "I hate the thought but she is a lonely vulnerable woman that hasn't been with a man in quite a while. You can put the last piece in place...for all of us."

"I dunno..." Ray replied. "I guess it's kinda of hard for me to believe you really want me to jump in bed with another woman?"

"I really don't Ray..." Marsha admitted. "But I know it will improve the quality of all of our lives. It almost seems as if it is destiny. Think about it Ray...we unwittingly conspired to liberate Kenneth and David. Freeing them to produce a large ranch with three beautiful houses. One for them, one for us and one we unknowingly restored for Cyndi, Kevin and Katelynn."

"So now it all boils down to me talking Cyndi into moving to the ranch," Ray replied.

"No, it boils down to whether or not you want two wives?" Marsha corrected.

"Two wives?" Ray questioned.

"That's what it will quickly become," Marsha advised.

"I don't know about this pumpkin," Ray responded. "I realize we came here because Cyndi is a threat to the way things are but do you really think this is the best way to handle it?"

"As much as I detest the thought of sharing you I truly believe this is the only real solution sweetheart," Marsha replied. "And I really hate that Ray because it puts you on the spot for everyone on the ranch," she continued.

"Well...I am the foreman," Ray chuckled. "And you really think Cyndi wants to sleep with me?" he questioned again.

"I know she does," Marsha responded. "You are a charming man Ray Jenkins. You can brighten and remake her entire world...just as you did mine. And in a real way I think she is entitled to that. And I know you are most certainly entitled to have two women…if you want them."

"Hum… two families on the same ranch means I would have to split my time," Ray suggested.

"I know and I hate thinking about it. So I have to concentrate on what I will be getting in return," Marsha pouted.

"You are some kind of woman and I love you pumpkin but I dunno," Ray responded as he parked the car, "I gotta sleep on this one."

Late the following morning Marsha was delighted to find Cyndi fully made up and wearing her sexy new housedress when she and Ray arrived. Cyndi fussed and fidgeted over Kevin and Katelynn for several minutes before making certain they were securely buckled into Marsha's rental car then hurried back into the house, not wanting to see them drive off.

"They couldn't be in better hands, believe me… they will be fine," Ray assured.

"I know. I mean I'm sure they will be okay…but they are my babies," Cyndi replied.

"Yeah I know and they are terrific kids which means you must be a great mom," Ray offered.

"Why thank you Ray. It's really nice of you to say that," Cyndi responded.

"Hey the truth is what it is," Ray smiled.

"Would you like some coffee or something?" Cyndi asked. "I only have ordinary coffee…sorry no cappuccino."

"That's cool, I like ordinary coffee, hot and strong," Ray responded then followed Cyndi to the kitchen where she brewed a fresh pot of coffee and wringed her hands.

"Hey now...don't worry yourself to death. Kevin, Katelynn and Marsha will all be fine," Ray again offered.

"Well...at least she left you for a hostage," Cindy replied with a smile as she poured two steaming cups of coffee then sat down at the breakfast table across from Ray.

Ray grinned because Cyndi had caught him in the act of sizing her up. She was shorter and heavier than Marsha was. Perhaps a few pounds overweight but had a terrific shape that more than filled the sexy housedress she was wearing. The dress was very low cut, open back, black silk and lace with the long slits on either side. Cyndi had carefully made herself up and looked absolutely delicious. Ray was caught studying the sensual moves of her body against the silk. "Umm... good coffee," he praised in between sips.

"So you are going to explain some legal offer or something?" Cyndi asked.

"Yeah...something like that," Ray responded. "Now don't misunderstand, I ain't no lawyer, I'm just telling you what Kenneth and David are willing to give up if you drop the lawsuit and promise never to file another one."

"Boy! This had better be good," Cyndi teased.

"Believe me baby, I done my best to make it as good as possible," Ray bragged.

"Okay let's hear it."

"Have you any idea just exactly where Kenneth and David live?" Ray inquired.

"Some little town in California. I can't remember the name but I got it wrote down. Why?" Cyndi responded.

"Because they live on a two hundred and seventy-three acre ranch, that's why!"

"A two hundred seventy-three acre ranch?" Cindy gasped.

"Exactly...and by the end of this year, it will be supporting itself and producing a profit. Part of that ranch belongs to you...if you want it," Ray advised.

"Wait! Who owns this ranch?" Cyndi asked.

"Kenneth and David own eighty percent of the real property and one hundred percent of the expenses. I am the foreman and Marsha and I own our house and twenty percent of the real property plus twenty percent of any and all net profits," Ray responded.

"What's my cut?" Cyndi asked.

"A beautiful house plus ten percent of the real property and net profits with no expenses," Ray answered.

"A house?" Cyndi questioned.

"Exactly!" Ray confirmed. "A carefree, expense free life on a great ranch which also happens to be a terrific place for your kids to grow up. There's even a stable close to the house so they could even have a pony...and they would get to see their father every so often. There are great schools nearby...public and private and it really is a cool old farmhouse. It's restored and empty just waiting for a family. Why don't you fly back with us and check it out?" he asked.

"Wait just a minute Ray! You're saying I should move to a ranch in California?"

"Why not Cyndi? It's a wonderful place to live. What's so great about here? Certainly not the cold ass winters. What you got to lose by coming to look? Marsha really wants you to,...and so do I!"

"Now let me get this straight Ray," Cyndi responded. "If I drop my lawsuit against Kenneth, I get ten percent of the ranch, a house, no expenses and everybody really wants me to move there."

"Now I didn't say everybody, I can't speak for Kenneth and David, but Marsha and I really want you to," Ray assured.

"I don't know Ray...this whole thing sounds suspicious to me. Why would Marsha want me to move onto that ranch?" Cyndi questioned.

"Because she is the only woman on the ranch and she is pregnant!" Ray replied.

"Pregnant?" Cyndi gasped. "Whoa! Wait a minute here I thought Marsha couldn't have kids."

"Yeah, that's what she told me when I first met her. But apparently it was the seed, not the soil that was the problem cause she is two months pregnant as we speak," Ray insisted.

"Well my...aren't you quite the stud?" Cyndi teased.

"I try my best!" Ray responded with a grin.

"Still," Cyndi continued, "I really don't see why I should leave my family and friends and move half way across the country where I hardly know anyone."

"What you got to lose by just checking it out? The truth is you will probably win a judgment against Kenneth in your lawsuit, but if he stays out of this state you will never collect one dime. On the other hand if you did move to the ranch, you won't have to hassle with trying to make ends meet. You and your kids will enjoy a great life and your friends and relatives will be more than happy to visit and stay longer than you want," Ray countered.

"And just who will be there for me when I need something?" Cyndi questioned.

"I will!" Ray replied.

"Oh yeah right...I'm sure Marsha is just going to give you to me whenever I happen to need something...huh?" Cyndi responded with cynicism.

"She gave me to you today didn't she?" Ray replied.

For several minutes Cyndi said nothing. She sipped her coffee, stared into Ray's eyes and found herself blushing. She stood up to get more coffee but leaned against the kitchen counter, looked out the window and begin wringing her hands.

Ray joined her at the counter and took her hands into his. "I'm here for you now and I'll be there for you on the ranch," he said softly.

"I don't know Ray, this is all so unexpected."

"Cyndi? Do you really have a happy and fulfilling life here?"

She searched his eyes for several moments then whispered, "No...Ray you have no idea of how downright awful and lonely my life has been. It's only gotten worse since David walked out...and I'm not sure I really want to see or be near him again," she confided.

"You won't have to," Ray assured, "there are three houses on that ranch and none of them are close to the other. Marsha and I have been there almost a year and we have only seen David three times and Kenneth once since we arrived. Marsha and I came here because your lawsuit could threaten a lifestyle we find very comfortable and are growing to love. Yesterday we realized you are the odd person out and should also be included. We also realized we really dig you and your kids. I really like you and we know the ranch is a perfect fit for all of us. I called David last night and renegotiated your deal because Marsha and I really want you there. Give the ranch a try Cyndi...if you don't like it, you don't have to stay," he promised.

"Do you really mean that Ray? You really like me?" Cyndi asked, her eyes sparkling.

Ray put his arms around Cyndi. "Yes! I like you a lot...and you like me too don't you?" he challenged.

"Yes," Cyndi whispered as she tilted her chin upwards and allowed Ray's lips to meet hers.

At first their lips gently pressed together but soon the kiss grew passionate and wet. Together they lustfully explored and savored the taste and touch of the other. After a few moments Ray made several attempts to break the kiss but Cyndi refused and began grinding her hips against him. Feeling the power of her urgent need, Ray massaged her back and got deeper and deeper into Cyndi's kiss until they sank to the kitchen floor.

Marsha meanwhile was enjoying one of the happiest days of her life. The fact that she was pregnant only made her maternal instincts stronger and she relished this opportunity to play mommy. Kevin and Katelynn eagerly obliged by clinging to her and asking nonstop questions. They were about half way through the petting zoo when Ray scooped Cyndi from the kitchen floor and carried her to bed.

It had been nearly three years since Cyndi had been with a man and that had been a half-hearted encounter with David. She overwhelmed Ray on the kitchen floor and had not broken the kiss until he entered her. When he did she cried out and wildly thrashed about. It took a few moments for Ray to gain control of her then make passionate love until Cyndi exploded in climax and begged for more.

In the bedroom the pace was slower and Ray was excited and very turned on by Cyndi but took his time. He had never expected to experience another woman after Marsha and knowing this woman would likely become his second wife now inflamed raw hunger and deep desires he didn't even know he had. Cyndi was totally different. Marsha was a beautiful, slim and classy brunette while Cyndi was cute, blonde and a little plump. In fact she was Ray's perfect second love. He eagerly shared the pleasures of sensual massage, oral sex and such unrestricted passion neither of them wanted it to end. Yet by the time Marsha and the kids returned Ray and Cyndi had showered, dressed and were sitting on the sofa chatting.

The following Monday Cyndi, Kevin and Katelynn joined Ray and Marsha on the flight to California. The kids instantly fell in love with the ranch and did not want to leave. But Cyndi was not so sure. She found the farmhouse very comfortable and inviting and liked the idea of living on the ranch but was not convinced they should actually move there. To give Cyndi time to really look things over and become comfortable with the move, Marsha took the kids to the ranch house and Ray spent two days and nights alone with Cyndi in the farmhouse. Then acting purely on a hunch, Ray borrowed a pony from the neighboring rancher. Much to his and Marsha's surprise, Cyndi knew how to ride and immediately began teaching her children, prompting Ray to buy two ponies and a mare for his new family.

The horses sealed the deal. Riding helped Cyndi relax and it allowed her to release her skepticism. For the first time in many years she found herself actually enjoying life. Three weeks later, Ray and Cyndi flew back to the Midwest. They put her house up for sale, packed and shipped her furniture and belongings to the ranch, then spent over a week on the road, driving Cyndi's minivan to California and really getting to know each other. By the time they reached Reno, Nevada they had known each other for only about a month but their deep attraction was blossoming into real love.

During her teenage years Cyndi was overweight and the subject of ridicule by the boys at school. As a result she was very shy and timid around men. Ray was only the third man Cyndi had known sexually and the first to lead her to climax. He claimed her totally by coming to her rescue, overwhelming her with passion then taking complete charge of her life. Even though she knew she could only share him, she absolutely adored Ray and quickly fell deeply in love. More in love than even she thought possible.

Ray was incredulous. Never in his life had he ever thought about having two wives. He wasn't really sure it was a good idea because without question Marsha was the true love of his life and always would be. Yet he liked Cyndi and was very attracted to her. He had entered into this relationship for the good of all, but was now surprised to find that he was truly falling in love with Cyndi.

Captured by the beauty of Lake Tahoe, Ray and Cyndi stayed for three days in a luxury hotel suite with a spectacular view of the lake. Three days of carefree play, relaxation and love that unmistakably had the look and feel of a honeymoon.

When they finally returned to the ranch, Ray and Cyndi were thrilled to find Marsha and the kids excited and happy to see them. Although he was very uneasy about the consequences, Ray confessed his growing love for Cyndi to Marsha then considered himself the luckiest man alive when Marsha expressed her approval.

"I knew it would come to this and I couldn't be happier!" Marsha assured him. "Now we have a perfect world. I have a great kid sister living nearby, we both have a terrific husband and we both have children that will grow up together on this wonderful ranch. Oh Ray, you don't know how perfect this really is," Marsha gushed.

"And you really don't mind when I spend a night or two with Cyndi?" Ray questioned.

"Honestly…I don't like spending the night without you, but you are her husband too and she misses and deserves you as much as I do," Marsha responded.

"Wait a minute now…I didn't marry Cyndi, I married you!" Ray insisted.

"Yes you did…and it was the happiest and most special day in my life," Marsha beamed. "You are mine and that will never change. I love you more than I ever knew I could love someone that's why I have no problem sharing you with Cyndi. I know she also needs and will enjoy you. I know you will enjoy her and still be there for me. You can't believe how hot I get after missing you for a couple of days and knowing you are with her," Marsha confessed.

"I have to admit you have been a tiger lately," Ray grinned.

"Ray! Sweetheart...don't you see this is destiny," Marsha advised. "There is no other woman on this planet I'm willing to let near you. Cyndi and I are sisters of the same tragedy...you are our rescuer. You saved both of us from a life of bitterness and despair. There is no way I cannot share you with her...and I think we should have a ceremony," she suggested.

"What kind of ceremony?" Ray quizzed.

"Why a wedding ceremony of course," Marsha replied with a big smile.

"Well much as I would like to accommodate, I already happen to be married and I ain't giving that one up," Ray smugly relied.

"I know you are married silly...it won't be an official wedding, just a meaningful one," Marsha advised. "One that means far more than official papers and processes. We should have it right here...oh my god Ray! I'm sorry...I've gotten completely carried away...it's up to you and Cyndi to decide if you want a ceremony...not me. I'm sorry sweetheart. It's all just so perfect I couldn't help myself," she apologized.

Ray chuckled and held Marsha tight in his arms. "You really are a special woman Marsha Jenkins and I truly love you...but we'll see about that ceremony business," he concluded.

It didn't take long before Ray found himself attempting to quiet Cyndi's fears about Marsha becoming jealous over the time he spent with her. Despite his assurances, Cyndi was not convinced until Ray offered to marry her in a mock but serious ceremony. Cyndi was delighted at his offer and on cloud nine when she learned it was really Marsha's idea.

The ceremony took place on the large front porch of the farmhouse. At Cyndi's insistence David gave her away and Kenneth reluctantly performed the role of the minister. To Ray's delight, both Kenneth and David found the whole matter uncomfortable and could not wait to get on their way. As soon as the ceremony and reception was over, Marsha took the kids to the ranch house and Ray spent the next two days secluded in the farmhouse with his new bride.

Less than one week later, Cyndi appeared at the local county courthouse where she legally changed her last name and the last name of her children from Rollins to Jenkins.

Chapter nine

Life on the ranch soon took on a familiar and comfortable rhythm. Cyndi planted a large vegetable garden close to her house and spent much of her days gardening then cooking for her kids and for Ray and Marsha. Occasionally she would cook enough for David and Kenneth then draft Ray to deliver it. Though they never admitted it, both David and Kenneth were overjoyed to get Cyndi's home cooked meals and anxiously looked forward to the next one. Marsha worked diligently at her computer, providing impeccable legal research for her employer, while Ray managed the ranch and successfully divided his time between his two families, frequently taking all of them on outings to the ocean or San Francisco.

Four years later Ray sat in his truck atop a ridge that overlooked much of the ranch. He scanned the terrain thinking of how much his life had changed in so short a time. The ranch was now everything to him. Under his direction it had quickly taken shape and now reliably produces a sizeable profit. It was home. A great home for his two beautiful families but Ray was troubled because David had called and asked him to come by the cabin. David never called unless something needed repaired and he always told Ray what the problem was during his call. This time David did not mention anything that needed to be fixed, he only asked him to drop by at a certain time.

On his last visit to the cabin to repair a deck railing, Ray arrived while David and Kenneth were entertaining several gay friends. The talk at that party which Ray overheard was all about how wonderful it would be if David and Kenneth turned the entire ranch into a gay retreat. Ray didn't think about that much until now as he sat in his truck and pondered the unknown. What would he do if David and Kenneth had decided to turn the ranch into a gay retreat? His wives would object and so would he. But together they only owned thirty percent and were powerless. As minority owners they could only sell out and move on, or try and fence off their eighty one plus acres and create a separate ranch. But that would be difficult since the ranch had a sizable mortgage on it.

Ray thought about his two separate families, each in their own house. Marsha had given birth to Ray Junior then two years later to Michael, while Cyndi with Kevin and Katelynn had given birth to Carolyn Marie and was now again pregnant with his child. Ray seriously doubted they could all live together in one house and the thought of moving them to the city was inconceivable. He needed the ranch, his families needed the ranch and they could not share it with endless streams of homosexual men running about.

Ray sighed deeply, started the engine and drove to the cabin. When he arrived he noticed David and

Kenneth sitting on the deck in front of the barbeque grill. Both had a stack of papers they threw one at a time into the fire. Onan moved between them. Onan was a young gay Asian man from San Francisco. For the past year he had spent most of his time on the ranch with Kenneth and David. He wore only a thong and each time Kenneth threw a paper on the fire Onan kissed him on the lips. When David threw a paper on the fire, Onan would kiss his bare chest. Ray sighed again and stepped from his truck.

"Hey Ray my man," David called out as Ray approached the deck. Kenneth gave his stack of papers to Onan and retreated inside.

"Come on over and have a seat," David invited. "Onan! Get the man a glass of champagne!" he ordered.

"Freeze that champagne!" Ray interrupted. "Make it bourbon or whisky, two fingers and one finger of cola."

"Oue...you such a real man!" Onan gushed.

Ray ignored him and looked around. The place was still in good shape. No railings loose, flooring in tact, roof still looks good. In the yard was a canvas draped over a very large object.

"Sit down Ray...sit down!" David insisted. "ONAN!" he called out.

"Coming...coming," Onan replied then rushed over with Ray's drink and the stack of papers.

Ray settled into a chair, sipped his drink and mentally prepared to hear the worst.

"Ray my man, we are celebrating!" David beamed. "Yes sir...my man I do mean celebrating. Sixteen business days ago I made the final installment on the mortgage...and today we received the deed and all the official paperwork. You hear me Ray...the ranch is paid for...free and clear. WE OWN IT!"

"You shittin me?" Ray quizzed.

"No sir! Never!" David insisted. "Thanks mostly to the profits from the ranch, which you have produced, and a little of the profit from our business we have paid the mortgage. Those papers you are holding are the mortgage documents and other now unimportant loan papers. This is a mortgage burning party...YEEE--HA!" David threw several papers in the fire and Onan promptly kissed his chest and licked his nipples. "Go ahead Ray...burn em...go ahead...it feels so good," he assured.

"And I will reward you!" Onan added.

Ray examined several of the documents, including the final statement of payment. "This really is on the level...huh?" he questioned.

"Absolutely!" David beamed. "We now own the ranch free and clear!"

"Well kiss my ass! I congratulate you for taking care of business the right way," Ray praised.

"Just following your clear lead sir," David replied. "You are the one that insisted on putting all the profits back into the ranch.

"Hum..." Ray concluded, after again satisfying himself the mortgage had really been paid in full. "Don't mind if I do burn a few of these sumbitches...but hold up on that reward shit son," he advised Onan.

"How can I please you?" Onan inquired. "I must do something for you. You big man on ranch!"

"Just stay yo ass over there somewhere and I'll be pleased with that," Ray replied.

"But I nice and smooth and soft too...nice smooth ass see?" Onan offered as he slowly turned around rolling his hips and sucking his fingers.

Ray ignored him and threw a handful of papers into the fire while Onan stood with his head hung down.

"Aw gee Ray you don't understand his culture, the poor guy is deeply offended and feels very inadequate by your rejection," David advised. "Why don't you let him give you a blowjob? He is among the best...and I should know!"

"No thanks," Ray responded.

"Well let him do something for you...any little thing," David pleaded.

"Hum...okay make me another drink, then take off my shoes and massage my feet. That good enough for you?" Ray asked.

Onan flashed a big smile, promptly made another drink, settled on the floor, removed Ray's shoes and slowly massaged his feet.

"Now we're living!" David responded with a wide grin. "And I got more news that's even better. When I finish telling you everything Ray you will be so happy Onan might get a taste of that legendary meat in your pants after all!" he chuckled.

"Yeah, we'll see about that!" Ray replied.

"You can't believe how happy I am Ray...we all are just overjoyed!" David beamed then called out. "KENNY? KENNY?"

Kenneth appeared at the door of the cabin.

"Come hear baby!" David beckoned. "You are not going to believe what I have to tell you Ray," he continued.

Kenneth approached and David pulled him into his arms and kissed him passionately before Kenneth settled on the floor and rested his head against David's thigh.

"Now here's the really good part. Kenneth and I have landed a major contract with a very large French pharmaceutical firm," David stroked Kenneth head as he talked. "We are going to design the software for a complete corporate computer conversion. Eight plants, twelve distribution centers, twenty-six offices plus corporate headquarters. It's a fantastic project...AND...we will have to live and work in Paris until it's finished. Two years at least. Isn't that great Ray? We got about five weeks to close up shop here and get to Paris. I am SO excited," David gushed.

"Hum...congratulations...I don't quite know what to say," Ray admitted.

"Don't say anything yet...there's lots more good stuff and this part you are really going to like," David replied.

Kenneth again quickly retreated into the cabin because he did not want to share this bit of news. This decision was the most severe disagreement he ever had with David. He gave in only because he loved David who was concerned for their basic security. David had complete trust in Raymond Jenkins and knew with this arrangement no matter what; he and Kenneth would always have their cabin, 54 acres and a modest expense free income. He loved Kenneth and forced this issue for their mutual long term well being.

"Now that the ranch is paid off," David continued, "and we are going to Paris for awhile, it is clearly the right time to redistribute the collective ownership of the ranch. So, I had the deed and all papers of ownership redrawn to reflect the following. Ah hem!" David paused, sipped his champagne then continued. "Ownership and clear title to this ranch is now divided into five shares. Marsha owns one share worth ten percent. Cyndi owns one share worth ten percent. Kenneth owns one share worth ten percent. I own one share worth ten percent, and you Mr. Jenkins own one share worth sixty percent. Now how do you like those apples?" he asked handing Ray the papers with a broad smile.

Ray was speechless as he studied the papers in disbelief, completely unaware of Onan sucking his toes.

"Hey that's not all!" David announced. "You'll notice in those documents we also changed the name of the ranch. The new name...ONAN!"

Onan sprang off the deck and hurried to the canvas-covered object in the yard.

"The new name is..." Onan pulled the canvas from the new ranch sign. "RENAISSANCE RANCH!" David announced in a loud happy voice.

"Renaissance Ranch?" Ray quizzed.

"Yes sir, Renaissance Ranch...how do you like it?" David asked.

"How do I like it? I'm not sure. What does it mean?" Ray asked.

Onan returned to the deck and knelt on the floor in front of Ray with worship in his eyes.

"Mr. Jenkins..." David grinned. "You are the man! Our liberator. Our true Renaissance Man! You made it possible for Kenny and me to be together. You took charge where we needed it most. You liberated us from our ex-wives, both of them, which made it possible for all of us to thrive and become successful. And...you have been one hell of a great dad to those kids I never wanted in the first place. You are the man, the Renaissance Man. Whether you like it or not, every time Kenny and I make love you are there with us. We couldn't be there at all without you being there first. You are master of our renaissance Mr. Jenkins and THIS is now officially Renaissance Ranch!"

Ray stumbled for words not knowing quite what to think.

"Perhaps now you understand why Onan wants to suck your cock so badly," David quietly explained.

Ray reclined in his chair. "Fix me another drink!" he ordered and Onan instantly responded.

"Hey now you can't have Onan too!" David teased. "He is going to Paris with us."

"I don't know what to say," Ray honestly replied.

"You don't have to say anything," David countered. "It's all a done deal anyway...and you have more than earned everything you got! But...if you want to do something really nice for me in return you could let Onan suck your cock. He truly believes you are a black god...and it would really be a very special experience for him...that's not a hell of a lot to ask is it Ray?"

"Damn I guess not," Ray concluded then slowly stood up and lowered his pants and shorts.

When Ray's big black cock sprang into view Onan bowed before it several times out of serious reverence and deep respect. This was the cock that was undefeated on the wrestling mat. This was the cock that first choked then deflowered Kenneth. This was the cock that twice impregnated a woman that had been declared barren and this cock continues to regularly satisfy two sexually demanding women. This was the big meaty dark chocolate cock that tamed the land and was the subject of continued high praise from David and Kenneth. Onan was clearly moved and in total awe of this man and his cock.

As Ray returned to his chair and made himself comfortable a completely naked Kenneth emerged from the cabin. He helped David from his shorts then eased onto his lap. They kissed and hugged each other then intently watched Onan nervously slide Ray's big black cock into his hot hungry mouth.

Although Onan was an experienced cocksucker, the taste and feel of Ray's cock in his mouth sent shivers of delight and excitement racing through his whole body. He performed well above his exceptional skill level with tears of joy pouring from his eyes, while Ray relaxed, closed his eyes and gave himself to the moment.

He opened his eyes when Kenneth suddenly tapped Onan on the shoulder and took his place. Kenneth sucked Ray with the passion of love and hate. It was he that first complicated the rhythm of life and eventually brought everyone to this place. He was delighted with his own gains and place in life, yet jealous and resentful of Ray. In spite of that fact or maybe because of it, Kenneth was deeply aroused and excited. He could have made Ray cum but David tapped him on the shoulder and took his place.

David did not often suck cock. In their gay world he was considered a top man, meaning he gave but rarely received. Yet for some time, the awe, gratitude and admiration he felt made him long to honor Ray, his Renaissance man, by kneeling before him and sucking his cock. Ray was a real man and among the few David truly respected. He sucked Ray for several long moments savoring both the taste and the experience before again taking Kenneth into his arms and allowing Onan the thrill of finishing what he started.

Ray was feeling especially good. The news of the day was unexpected but could not have been better. The liquor had relaxed him and under the circumstances he really didn't mind letting Kenneth and David suck his dick. They had never made any secret of their desire to service him and up to now he had no interest or particular reason to allow it.

Onan was a different story. Ray permitted this blowjob only out of gratitude to David but found himself impressed. Onan's lips, mouth, tongue and throat muscles all seem to be working on his dick at the same time. Ray would never openly admit it but he liked Onan and would have kept him as a houseboy if things were different. His dick throbbed hard and felt powerful as Onan sucked with great skill and enthusiasm. To Ray's amazement his entire dick repeatedly disappeared inside the young Asian boy's mouth. Delighted he grabbed the back of Onan's head and truly fucked his face. Onan's nose was buried in Ray's crotch hair and he was sucking with a wet, fiery hunger when Ray's cock violently jerked in orgasm. Semen slid down his throat while tears streamed from Onan's eyes as he sucked Ray dry and kept sucking. Onan wanted to keep this cock in his mouth forever and was overjoyed that Ray held his head and continued to fuck his mouth, finally slowing to a stop but keeping his cock in Onan's mouth. It was the best blowjob of Ray's life and he truly enjoyed it.

Kenneth knelt and sucked David's cock for a few moments then lay face down on the deck. David straddled him, pushed his cock into Kenneth's ass and they fucked vigorously while Ray and Onan watched. After a few minutes they rolled onto their side and motioned for Onan who quickly let Ray's cock slip from his mouth. He stood and bowed before Ray several times then removed his thong and stretched out opposite Kenneth. He slipped his small cock into Kenneth's mouth and sucked Kenneth's into his, all while David continued to slowly pump his cock in and out of Kenneth's ass.

Ray briefly watched them then put on his pants, collected his papers and said goodnight. He was amazed when the three men stopped their sexual activity and in unison said, "Good night Mr. Jenkins."

"And thank you Mr. Jenkins…I truly mean that! THANK YOU SIR! This has been a perfect partnership in every way," David added.

"Indeed it has," Ray agreed. "Indeed it has!"

On his way home, Ray slowly drove across a high ridge on the ranch watching the setting sun as it cast a golden glow over the land…his land. It had been a long and perhaps unusual journey, requiring him to shoulder a mighty load but he and his two families had arrived…and they were here to stay.

On the other side of the ranch, Marsha stepped out of the house and took a seat on her front porch to admire the sunset, just as Ray stopped his truck at the highest point on the ridge then settled back into the seat and smiled. Marsha did the same while a calm serene peace simultaneously settled over both of them. Far from each other's presence, without a word spoken, deep within their hearts both knew that the last of their burdens had lifted...the unknown was now known. The complications were gone...and the rhythms now play a beautiful melody.